HyperLinkz

Web Jam

BOOK 3 ROBERT ELMER

WATERBROOK
PRESS

WEB JAM
PUBLISHED BY WATERBROOK PRESS
2375 Telstar Drive, Suite 160
Colorado Springs, Colorado 80920
A division of Random House, Inc.

Unless noted in "The Hyperlinkz Guide to Safe Surfing," all Web-site names are fabrications of the author.

ISBN 1-57856-749-1

Published in association with the literary agency of Alive Communications, Inc., 7680 Goddard Street, Suite 200, Colorado Springs, CO 80920.

Library of Congress Cataloging-in-Publication Data has been requested.

Printed in the United States of America
2004—First Edition

10 9 8 7 6 5 4 3 2 1

Contents

Introducing... *Web Jam* 1

1   Dead Last 3

2   Hoity-Toity 10

3   Jessi 2 the Rescue 16

4   Pop-Up Mania 21

5   My Cyberhero 25

6   FAQ Jr. 31

7   *www.FannyCrosbyHymns.com* 38

8   Un-American Shopping Girls 45

9   Online Jammin' 50

10   Web Lessons 55

11   Follow the Links 60

12   Not Alone? 65

13   Jailhouse Rock 72

14   Virtual Rumble 78

15   Digital Plunge 84

16   Rockets' Red Blare 90

17   Virtual Wrigley 95

18   Grand Slam 101

19   Three-Minute Warning 107

20   Clueless Judges 112

The Hyperlinkz Guide to Safe Surfing 118

Introducing...Web Jam

Hey, Austin T. Webster here. Hardly anybody believes my sister, Ashley, and me when we try to explain what it's like to be sucked into the Internet, to actually step into a Web site where everything looks real, only it's not. We're talking actually *being* online, not just looking at it on a computer.

You don't believe me either? I don't blame you. But that's what happened in the past two adventures, *Digital Disaster* and *Fudge Factor.* No kidding. How was I supposed to know that taking a picture of my sister with a digital camera hooked to my laptop would feed her straight into the Internet?

I know that sounds totally off the wall, but I'm sure you can understand that I didn't want my sister to get hurt. That's why I followed her—that and to look for our aunt's prize-winning beagle, Applet. Did I mention Applet was the first one to be sucked into the Web?

Anyway, once there, we found ways to jump from site to site by stepping on hyperlinks, sometimes on purpose and other times not. On the way we met lots of…well, actually, they weren't real people, just Internet copies. How do I know? My sister asked one of them if he was a famous person. He

said, "This is a Web site, you know. I'm like an actor. No ⟨
is real here, except perhaps you and your brother."

But when you're trapped on the World Wide Web,
doesn't matter whether people or things are only copies; you
still trapped. Of course we figured out a way back home in ⟨
end. We e-mailed ourselves as attachments, which worked▌
sorta kinda. I got home to my laptop fine. Ashley ended up
the Normal Public Library computer room and had to w
home. Oh well.

I'm still working on some of my camera and computer s
tings. But hey, I don't want to tell you everything that's alrea
happened, just explain enough so you won't go "huh?" or
we jump into this next adventure.

So…are you hanging on to something?

CHAPTER 1

Dead Last

"Whoa!" Ashley Webster held her breath as a tall eighth grader sat down in front of the piano and unfolded his legs. Everyone else in the Chiddix Junior High auditorium that July Saturday morning seemed to be holding their breath too.

That came to about 750 other people holding their breath—moms and dads and friends and teachers and news reporters—and that was a lot of breath to hold. Finally, Ashley leaned over and whispered in her Aunt Jessica's ear.

"He's really good."

Jessi nodded her head and let her long blond hair swing to hide her face. "Not as good as you, Ash."

"Shh." Ashley wasn't so sure of that, listening to the way he played and sang "My Heart Will Go On," the tearjerker from the *Titanic* film.

When he reached the part about how safe his true love would be in his heart or wherever, some of the ladies sitting nearby started dabbing their eyes. Even Jessi was looking a little misty eyed. It was no accident that this kid from Peoria was one of the top ten finalists in the annual Greatest Young Vocalist Competition, the final ninety-minute sing-off between kids from all over the state.

After all the tryouts and practices and semifinals, it all came down to this: ninety minutes of do or die. One last chance to prove who was the best junior singer in the state of Illinois. And right here in Ashley's hometown of Normal, where two of the finalists lived.

Right now the boy on stage had as good a chance as anybody to win the prize: a brand-new Yamaha keyboard and a spot in the televised national Greatest Young Vocalist Competition.

Never mind the national competition, although taking part in that would be pretty cool. But the keyboard! A Yamaha professional stage piano, just like the pros used, with a full eighty-eight keys, a sixteen-track song recorder, and a MIDI computer interface. The one Ashley had been dreaming about every night for the past month. Ashley already had a place picked out for it in the living room of the house she lived in with her dad and mom and brother, Austin, on Fell Avenue.

But if she didn't win the keyboard, she couldn't take piano lessons. (Well, maybe she could use a piano at church, but her parents would have to drive her there, and she wouldn't be able to use it as often.) And if she couldn't take piano lessons, she'd have no chance at a college music scholarship. No college scholarship… Well, she wasn't going to think like that. All that was standing between Ashley and her planned future were the nine other finalists, and if all of them were as good as Mr. Peoria here…

She traced her finger down the list in her program, looking for proof she still had a chance, at least on paper.

There she was, performer number ten—dead last on the list, though hopefully that was because her last name started with a *W*. If they kept to the schedule, she'd be standing up there an hour and fifteen minutes from now, close to 11:25. Ashley Marie Webster, grade seven, will sing an oldie-but-goodie country pop song by Faith Morgan. Jessi had convinced her it would be exactly the kind of song the judges would like best. Never mind that Ashley didn't like "Cry Me a Flash Flood." She just hoped she wouldn't have to use the cheat sheet that had the words on it.

Speaking of cheat sheets, where is it?

Ashley checked her pockets, wondering, sweating. All she found was a pencil stub from mini golf, which was kind of weird because she never kept junk in her pockets. She checked behind her on the cushy foldup seat, and then under their feet.

"Would you relax?!" Jessi whispered in her ear.

"Easy for you to say," Ashley whispered back.

Jessi wasn't the one who would be making a fool of herse
up there in front of all these people, blowing her whole future
because she couldn't remember the first line.

"What?"

Ashley was about to repeat herself when she noticed th
tiny earphone in Jessi's ear that wiggled as Jessi chewed he
gum. She should have known. Either her aunt was in th
Secret Service or a hidden MP3 player was cranking out th
latest contemporary Christian boy-band hit.

"Forget it." Ashley waved her hand. *I'll just suffer quietly.*

They really weren't making much noise, but Jessi's fathe
glanced over with a look that said "shh."

Jessi's father, Ashley's grandfather. *Aunt* Jessica. Ashley ha
had to explain it plenty of times, since even though Jessi trul
was Ashley's aunt, she was only a few months older tha
Ashley and not quite thirteen. Weird, but true. Jessi wa
Ashley's mom's way-little sister.

Meanwhile the kid from Peoria finished his song, and th
crowd let loose.

"I still say you're a better singer." Jessi didn't sound as con
vinced as she clapped.

Now it was up to the five judges seated at the VIP tabl
at the front of the auditorium: The mayor of Normal, th
Honorable Francine Wurstheim, wearing her permasmile an
a businesslike blue suit; Dr. Manny Weaver, a round-face

music professor who combed his three hairs sideways over the top of his head; two music teachers from the Chicago area Ashley had never heard of before; and, rounding out the quintet, Normal's sort-of celebrity, Nick Francisco, who used to be the drummer for a groovy sixties band named Pink Pigeon Peace.

So far the judges seemed really polite, not at all like the ones on that *American Superstar* show. They would probably be saying things like "I really admire your effort and enthusiasm" or "That's a really cheery-looking outfit you're wearing." But right now Ashley couldn't bear to hear their reviews. She had to find somewhere to relax. Good thing she'd chosen a seat near the back so she could bail without anybody noticing. With the mayor saying a few words about the competition, now was the perfect time.

"Be right back," she told Jessi, but Aunt Jessi was already on her heels. That was a good thing, considering who showed up outside the ladies' room while Ashley was taking a sip from the drinking fountain.

"He was so-so," came a voice from behind her. "Don't you think?"

"So-so?" Ashley stood up straight and tried not to cough. "I thought he was really good."

Seeing Tucker Campbell right now made Ashley ill. When Tucker flashed her perfect white smile, it wasn't hard to see how Chiddix Junior High's most gorgeous girl had won every Little Miss Illinois contest she'd entered since fourth grade. Looks, poise, talent, a beautiful voice—Tucker knew she had it all.

"That's nice of you to say"—Tucker kept her I've-already-won smile glued to her perfect face—"but you know he really doesn't have a chance."

"I wouldn't be so sure."

Tucker dabbed at her lips with a tissue she handed off to her friend Amy Templeton.

"Well, I just don't want you to feel too disappointed when I win. You're okay with that, aren't you? At least you can play ball."

Jessi was right there to stand up to the put-downs, popping in between them like a boxing referee. "Ashley made girls' all-state last year."

"She should be sure to tell that to the judges when it's her turn. If people don't have enough talent to compete, anything helps, you know."

"Ashley doesn't need any help." Jessi stuck out her chin. "She's going to win this thing and the keyboard, all the way to the big show in New York."

Tucker threw back her perfectly highlighted blond hair and laughed. "My mother is already planning our trip. Lots of luck."

Ashley felt her face turn red, redder than it did when she wanted to slug Austin for changing the channel in the middle of a program she was watching. She held her tongue but knew what she would have said. *Not this time, Little Miss Illinois. That keyboard has my name on it!*

CHAPTER 2

Hoity-Toity

"Okay, just one more photo here." Austin hunched over his laptop and dragged a small box into place on the screen. The new masterpiece Web site he was creating for his sister, *www.AshleyWebster.com*, was almost ready to go live on the Internet. Only a few more pictures to place and...

"There you are!" called Jessi.

Phooey. Jessi must have spotted him from down the empty hall—empty, of course, on account of the fact that it was 10:15 on a Saturday morning and the Young Super-Dupe Competition, or whatever it was called, was the only thing going on.

"We've been looking for you all over the school!"

"Just finishing up this page. I won't miss Ashley's song." Austin tapped the last graphic into place, a cartoon of a bird with an envelope in its beak. Whenever somebody clicked on the bird, it would flap its wings and the envelope would open and close. Pretty cool.

"Yeah," said Jessi, "but while you were hiding here at the other end of the school, playing with your computer, I had to help your sister fight off Little Miss Illinois."

"Fight her off?" Austin squinted at his aunt from over the top of his computer screen. He might need glasses one of these days to see far-off things better. Someone who looked like Ashley leaned back against the locker wall and lowered herself to the carpeted floor next to him.

"Not really fight her off," Ashley explained. "She's just a little…"

"High and mighty." Jessi filled in the blank.

Ashley opened her mouth, but Austin asked another question before she could say anything.

"You think so, Jessi?"

"Yeah. Hoity-toity. Cocky. You know."

"I hear you." Austin kept working as he talked. "I just didn't know Tucker Campbell was like that. Are you sure we're talking about the same person? I thought she was nice."

"Nice as a snake." Jessi stuck out her tongue and hissed at Ashley, grabbing her playfully by the throat in what had to be a Tucker imitation. "The competition is mine, all mine. Now look into my eyes and turn to stone! Ah-ha-ha!"

"Stop it." Ashley pulled away.

"Well"—Jessi wasn't done—"it makes me wish I could sing so *I* could bring her down a notch or two."

"You can sing!"

"Yeah, right. I shop. You sing." Jessi made a face at Ashley and leaned over to see what Austin was doing.

She gave him a sideways look. "Hey, I thought you were supposed to be watching the control booth."

"I am. See?" He clicked on his screen, and it switched to a view of the stage. Their principal, Mr. Hayward, was introducing singer number two. All the controls and buttons of the light board showed at the bottom of the screen. Austin selected one of them to bring up the red and blue spotlights a bit.

"Cool." At least Jessi seemed impressed. "You can control everything in the auditorium from your laptop?"

He nodded. "Almost, but actually Drew is right there in the control booth doing all the work. Maybe they thought that was a better idea since his sister isn't singing."

That would be Drew Scarola, the only other guy at Chiddix Junior High who knew as much about computers and high-tech stuff as Austin did. No wonder they were friends.

"See?" He pointed. "I can even turn the main lights on and off."

"Like this?" Jessi touched the screen before Austin could stop her. The lights blinked, and Principal Hayward looked around.

"Well…er…" Mr. Hayward seemed to be looking straight at them as his words came through the laptop speakers. "I trust Mr. Scarola and Mr. Webster still have things under control. For our next number…"

"Don't touch things you don't understand," Austin warned Jessi.

"Sorry. But can you do anything else from here?"

"Everything a regular computer can do. Maybe more, since I'm hooked up to the wireless network here at school."

"Cool." Jessi got that glazed look in her eyes that usually meant she needed him to explain.

"That means I can e-mail from my laptop or surf the Web even while I'm walking around the halls. No wires as long as I'm inside the school. Kind of like using a cell phone instead of a home phone.

"See, look." Austin fiddled with the controls. "If I'm on the way to music class and need some quick info on…well, whatever, I can go to a music encyclopedia site."

Austin went on showing them around the Web site, only noticing the wide-eyed look on his sister's face when Jessi grabbed Ashley by the shoulders. "What's wrong with you? You're turning colors!"

"Thanks a lot." Ashley was shaking. "Just what I need to hear."

But Jessi was right. All of a sudden Ashley didn't look so good. She held a hand to her sweaty forehead and leaned against a locker.

"You're just worried about singing in front of everybody," Jessi told her. "Here, why don't you—"

"Uh-uh." Ashley shook her head. "That's not it. I feel the same way as when we went into the Internet the first time. Austin?"

"Hey, don't look at me." He held up his hands. "I haven't done anything."

"Are you sure?" Ashley held her head as it seemed to fade in and out. "The last thing I want is to get stuck on the Internet again."

"Yeah, and right in the middle of the—" Jessi was probably about to say "contest," but Ashley flickered and flashed exactly as the lights in the auditorium had a minute ago. "Whoa! Did you see that?"

Ashley's eyes grew bigger and rounder as she looked at her hands. "What's happening to me, Austin?"

"I don't know," he said. "Maybe some of the effects from the digital camera and the laptop that took us into the Web the first time still haven't worn off."

"Like when I got the flu last winter and it wouldn't go away for a month afterward?" asked Jessi.

Ashley groaned while Austin looked down at his laptop. Suddenly he slapped his cheek with the palm of his hand.

"Wait a minute," he told them. "The wireless connection! Maybe you're caught in the beam that connects me to the Internet." He scrambled to his feet. "Try standing over there."

Ashley danced around the hallway, looking for a safer spot, but it was like trying to escape an angry swarm of bees. They were going to find her no matter what. She totally disappeared for a second before blinking back into view long enough for Jessi to run toward her.

"Don't touch me!" Ashley held out her hand to stop Jessi from getting any closer. "You don't want to catch what I have."

"We'll get you back out, Ashley!" Austin hammered on his keyboard to try to close the connection, but not soon enough. Ashley flickered once more and was gone...for good.

CHAPTER 3

Jessi 2 the Rescue

"Oh dear!" Jessi ran over to where Ashley had last stood and carefully waved her hand through the air just to be sure Ashley wasn't there. (What would she have done if she'd bumped into bits and pieces of Ashley?) But Ashley was as gone, gone, gone as if she had never been standing there. And Austin was crumpled against the wall, rocking back and forth on his knees, his head in his hands.

"All my fault," he groaned softly. "I should have known something like this would happen."

Jessi paced around the spot where Ashley had digitized, trying to think of what to do. What would she do if Ashley had fallen into a lake and was drowning? Well, that would never happen, of course, since Ashley was one of the strongest swimmers she knew and had ribbons hanging all over her bedroom wall to prove it. Jessi could hardly dog-paddle.

But never mind the ribbons. Ashley needed her help.

"I should have grabbed her before she disappeared." Jessi crossed her arms and paced. "Wouldn't that have been the thing to do? What would have happened, Austin?"

"Probably you would have gone with her. That's how we went from site to site the last time. Someone holds on to you, and you both go to the same site. It works just like the transporter on *Star Trek*."

"I've never seen *Star Trek*."

Austin shrugged.

"But I should have grabbed her." Jessi rubbed her forehead. "I really should have."

"No," Austin frowned. "Ashley was right. We can find her better from right here on my laptop than we can chasing her around the Internet. And once we find her, I think I can show her how to get back."

"You mean she doesn't know?"

He shook his head no. "I've been messing with the settings."

"Okay, but she's my niece. I have to do something."

It didn't take Jessi long to decide what. This was a lot easier than going to the mall and trying to choose between cherry-metallica and plum-pudding nail polish.

"I'm going after her," she announced.

"No, you're not. You'll just get lost in there."

"I've decided. I'm going. And you can't stop me."

Arms crossed, she planted herself in front of Austin as if daring him to tell her no a second time.

He glanced up at her. "Go ahead then."

Jessi paused for a moment. The sound of cheers echoed down the hall in their direction. She blinked.

"You're going to help me, aren't you?" she finally asked.

"No way."

"You have to. She's your sister. Do you want her to be stuck on the Internet all by herself?"

"No"—at last Austin's shoulders fell, and he sighed—"but that doesn't mean we need to go flying in after her."

"Look," she told him, "you don't have to go. You can stay out here and do whatever you were going to do to bring her back. But it might happen faster if I go in after her. We need to find her in time to sing in the contest."

He started to say something, then he must have changed his mind.

"You have any better ideas?" Jessi asked.

Austin slowly dug into his tech bag for his digital camera and the cables to link it to the laptop. Then he stopped. "Wait a minute. What about Papa Reuben and Mama Wallis?"

Everyone called them Papa and Mama since it would be sort of strange to call Jessi's mom and dad Grandma and Grandpa, even though they were.

"What about them?" Jessi shrugged.

"They're going to be worried. What am I going to tell them?"

"You won't have to tell them anything. First of all, they won't even know I'm gone. They're always too busy chasing Colby."

Colby was Jessi's seven-year-old foster brother, who was going to have a hard time sitting still for the whole program.

"And second of all," she went on, "you'll have us back in time for Ashley's turn to sing, right?"

That would be in a little more than an hour from now. Jessi went on with her pep talk. She could talk her nephew into just about anything.

"We can't let Tucker Campbell win, right?"

"Right," Austin agreed.

"And third, you can find two people easier than one, right?"

"I'm not so sure about that."

"I am. You're smart." She closed her eyes. "Now snap my picture before something terrible happens to Ashley. Send me to the same place. You do know where that is, right?"

Did Austin know where his sister had gone?

"Sure, I do." Austin nodded at Jessi and checked the screen of his laptop. He was pretty sure. Mostly.

He cabled the camera to the laptop the way he'd done before, all the while wondering if it was still going to work. If Jessi was worried, she wasn't showing it. But that's just the way she was.

"Do I need to smile?" she asked, looking into the camera.

He leveled and focused, finger on the shutter button. "Doesn't matter. Just hold still."

The camera twittered for a moment, and then a red light blinked...and Jessi still stood in front of the door to room 122.

"Double cheese," she said, pulling up the corners of her mouth with two fingers for good measure. Nothing happened.

"Don't go wandering around when you get there," Austin told her as he fiddled with the camera. *A faster shutter speed might do the trick. What were the settings from last time?* "Anyway, just hang tight at the *Musicpedia* Web site until I find you."

And then what?

"Yes sir," she saluted. "Cheese!"

Austin squeezed the shutter once again. And this time when Austin looked up from the camera, his aunt Jessi had disappeared. No poof. No cloud of smoke or flash of light.

She was just gone.

Now he had a big job: to get both girls back before Ashley missed her turn to perform in—he checked his watch—just under an hour, and before anybody else missed them. Oh, and check in on Drew to make sure the sound system was still working the way it was supposed to. As Austin switched back to his auditorium cam, he heard a noise from down the hall.

A giggle.

CHAPTER 4

Pop-Up Mania

🖱

"This is it?" Jessi spun around, her head back, taking it all in. "I thought you said you could meet people and visit different places on the Internet. Cool events, fashion sites, virtual shopping—"

"Actually, we're not there quite yet."

As far as Ashley could tell, they were stuck in some kind of portal site, one of those places that opened to everything else on the Web. And since Jessi had arrived, it looked as if they'd stepped inside a huge red tent, except the floor was lighted with bright yellow lettering.

"Don't step on anything!" Ashley warned Jessi. "I see links all over the place."

"Links that will take me to other places?"

"Yeah, but if you step on one of them, I might not be able to catch up with you fast enough."

Jessi skipped along beside a giant row of letters, much too

close for Ashley's comfort. "If I stepped on this link, would it really take me to *www-dot-TheBeatlesOnline-dot-com* the way it says?"

"Probably. But look, we can't just go diving in, no matter how fun it might look. We have to wait right here for Austin to find us, remember? Didn't you tell me he said to stay put?"

"Hmm, yeah. But he's too slow."

"Just remember, time moves faster here on the Web than back in Normal."

Now Jessi was tiptoeing through the portal site the way people do in a cemetery, keeping to the pathways.

Suddenly Ashley heard a sound like a cork popping or a can of soda opening after someone has shaken it.

POP!

"Hey, Ashley!" Jessi's call echoed through the red haze. "You've got to see this!"

Ashley was already hurrying toward the popping as it sounded again and again.

POP! POP!

Jessi pointed to the growing crop of signs springing up around her. Some were as large as front doors, while others were as big as garage doors. Some bright, colorful signs sported flashing lights, some had pictures of musical instruments, and all had messages like *Special Offer! Five CD Favorites for Five Cents!* or *Your Source for Bargain Instruments. Click Here.*

One of the signs bobbed in front of their faces; another orbited them like a hungry dog.

Ashley lowered her voice, hoping to keep any more signs from popping up.

"Back out of here slowly," she whispered. "Watch where you step."

Bam! Too late. Another pop-up nailed Jessi squarely on the back, sending her flying. Good thing Ashley had hold of her hand. But that didn't help much when a fourth sign about the size of a dining-room table sprang up from below, hooking Jessi just behind the knee and dragging her with it, upside down.

"Whoa!" Jessi hung on, but she hadn't exactly been an upside-down monkey-bars champion back in grade school.

Right side up, Ashley let go of Jessi's hand and grabbed the top of the pop-up. And the weird part: They both swung right back into the pop-up—it was like peeking into a symphony orchestra pit—and back out again.

Inside the window they were blasted with *Ta-da, oom-pah, waaa-ahhh, BANG!* At least a dozen instruments played right in their faces, each one with a bright price tag attached. "Act now!" yelled a voice over the instruments. "Supplies are limited!"

Back outside, Ashley and Jessi caught their breath—until they swung back inside.

Woogah, woogah, maow-wao-PHHHTTT! A line of trom-bones aimed straight for their eardrums.

And finally back outside again. Jessi was sure getting a tas of what the World Wide Web was all about.

"How do we get rid of these pop-ups?" she asked.

"See that tiny box up in the far corner?" Ashley pointed a square in the pop-up's frame, close to Jessi's knees. "Ju knock on it as hard as you can."

Jessi rocked up and reached way out, but her face and ne were turning beet red from hanging upside down. Or mayt it was from the red light.

Well, it was a nice idea.

"Swing out a little more," Ashley coached her. Easy for h to say! "Almost there."

In another four swings, they had it. But actually clickir on the target turned out to be the simple part. The harder pa was feeling the pop-up disappear and falling to the red floor o their tailbones.

Now the pop-ups were exploding like popcorn in a m crowave turned on High, sometimes coming up through th floor, other times out of nowhere.

Ashley and Jessi crouched together, hanging on to eac other's hands.

That is till Jessi rolled to the side as another pop-up a sprouted beneath her.

CHAPTER 5

My Cyberhero

It turned out that the giggle at the end of the hall belonged to a girl—and not just any girl.

"Wow," Tucker Campbell said to Austin. "I saw it, but I'm not sure I believe it. That was a very cool trick, whatever you did."

She made the same inspection Jessi had, walking back and forth across the spot where Jessi had been standing, waving her hand, searching for the trapdoor that had to be there.

"Wish it was a trick," Austin answered, trying to concentrate on what he was typing.

Tucker even opened a half-dozen nearby lockers, which she could do, this being summer break. And every couple of seconds she would look over at Austin.

"So how'd you do it? I saw your sister, and then...then..."

"Jessi."

"Right. I saw her disappear too. But no smoke and no mirrors."

"That's 'cause there aren't any." Austin tried to concentrate. "It's not a magic trick."

"Then what is it?"

He looked up at Tucker, and she sure didn't look like…whatever it was Jessi had said.

"Come on, Austin, you can tell me. We were buddies in Mr. Frazier's history class, weren't we?"

Buddies? He remembered she had asked him for a piece of gum once. Juicy Fruit. She'd told him thanks. If that counted as being buddies, then okay.

"Uh…" Austin swallowed hard as she sat down on the floor next to him. It was pretty clear she wanted to see what he was doing, though of course by this time the screen was filled with HTML code, a strange combination of words and characters that looked like this: *img src="music.jpg" alt="Ashley Webster's Web Page" width=250 height=140 align="right."* HTML code is what Austin used to build Web sites.

Pretty exciting stuff.

He sighed. "Okay, but you have to promise not to tell anybody."

"I get it." She smiled a perfect smile, showing her perfect teeth. She'd gotten her braces off way ahead of everyone else in school. "Magician's secrets."

"Not really." He pointed at the laptop. "Ashley and Jessi are in there."

Tucker squinted at the screen as if she were trying to understand an algebra problem in Mr. Pizzaro's Integrated Math I class. One of those problems that filled the chalkboard with lots of x's and y's.

"In there?"

"Actually, no. Not 'in there' as in 'inside my laptop.' I shouldn't have said it that way. But they've been digitized...like everything else you see on the Internet. I know it sounds weird, but my sister's lost somewhere on the Internet."

Tucker laughed long and hard.

"So..." She mopped a tear from her eye. "Is she, like, *alive?*"

"Oh yeah. She's fine. But she got there accidentally. And then Jessi went in after her on purpose."

"Whatever." Tucker lifted her eyebrows. "So where are they really hiding?"

"I'm telling you the truth. You saw what happened. They're gone."

Tucker looked around one more time, shaking her head.

"Okay," she told him at last. "So...let's just say you're right about this. Don't you need to tell somebody, like Mr. Hayward?"

"Are you kidding? I can hardly get *you* to believe me, and

you saw everything. Mr. Hayward doesn't even know how to work his e-mail."

"Well, yeah, but you said Ashley's lost, didn't you? And now Jessi, too?"

"Actually, it's not a big deal. They probably know where they are. I just haven't been able to log on to the right site yet. The server's cranky."

"Whatever that means."

"A server's a supercomputer that helps run the Internet. They're all over the place. Chicago, New York, San Francisco, Tokyo—"

"Okay, I get it." She got back to her feet. "So if your sister and Jessi are on the Internet, how do you get them back?"

"That's what I'm working on. Like I said, first I have to find them."

"But that could take awhile?"

"I hope not. But maybe."

Tucker twirled her highlighted hair around a finger.

"Well, that would be terrif—ible. Terrible. If your sister missed her time to sing, I mean."

Austin checked his watch again.

"I'm trying to work fast. But Internet time and our time aren't always the same. Like in *The Lion, the Witch, and the Wardrobe,* you know? Years go by in Narnia, and then the kids come back home, and it's been only a few minutes."

"I've never read that book"—Tucker stared over Austin's shoulder at the screen—"but you must be really smart to figure out all this computer stuff."

Austin felt the back of his neck getting warm. He shrugged. "Lots of people do this."

"Nobody I know."

She let each word drop as if with a little thud. Which, when he thought about it, was exactly what his heart was doing at that moment. *THUD-thud.* Wow! The temperature seemed to go up a couple more degrees, and he pulled at the collar of his Chiddix Chargers T-shirt. Maybe the air conditioning hadn't been turned on in this part of the school building.

"Well, anyway"—Austin tried to think of something smart to say—"I'd better get back at it."

The double doors at the end of the hallway flew open, and a mom checked them out with zoom vision, the way moms do.

"Tucker, honey?" That would be Tucker's mom. "They're on singer number three now. You're number four. You really need to be warming up, dear."

Tucker cleared her throat and sang a couple of perfect *la-la-la-la*'s.

"Be right there, Mom."

Her mom looked at Austin the same way she might look at a stray dog. Tucker stood up and smiled once more.

"Good luck finding them. I mean, I'd hate to see Ashley miss her turn."

Austin nodded and hoped she hadn't noticed that his glasses were steaming up.

CHAPTER 6

FAQ Jr.

Ashley did her best to steer clear of the musical pop-up ads, but it was no good. One hit her on the elbow, another bumped her shoulder, while a third buzzed in her ear. Just then a teenage guy stumbled in out of the red mist and tripped right in front of them.

"Yikes!" Ashley wasn't sure what was worse, the crazy pop-ups or…this guy.

He wore faded black jeans and one of those black-and-white T-shirts with a tuxedo printed on the front. His hair stuck out every which way.

"Man," he groaned. "You have no idea how hard you were to find."

Ashley backed up a step. "Who was looking?"

"Oh yeah. Sorry." He slowly got to his feet and dusted himself off. "This is my first time out alone. Dad says I'm supposed to introduce myself to new clients."

Jessi looked over at Ashley before asking, "Do we look like clients?"

"You do when you ask questions." The guy bowed stiffly, as if he'd never done it before. He went a little off balance, then caught himself.

"My dad's tied up at the moment; server's overloaded. He sent me to help."

"That was nice of him." Ashley still wasn't sure what to think. "But who are you?"

"Oh, me? You can call me FAQ Jr. Little FAQ. Son of FAQ. Take your pick. I've heard them all."

For a moment Ashley almost felt sorry for the guy. He looked so eager and clueless at the same time—sort of like Jessi. This was the son of the Internet butler, Mr. FAQ? The dapper man in the tuxedo who could instantly answer almost any question in the world?

"I think he's kind of cute," Jessi whispered to her.

Ashley hoped he hadn't heard. *How embarrassing!*

"He's just an Internet character, Jessi," she whispered back.

"So what do you do...er...Junior?" Jessi asked.

He stood up straighter, then looked down at his palm, where he had scribbled a few notes.

"Well, my job is to take all your questions, since FAQ stands for Frequently Asked Questions. And then I'll tell you I don't know the answer."

"You don't know any answers at all?" Ashley said in surprise. *What good is he, then?*

"Well, I can tell you to restart your computer. If that doesn't help your problem, you should reinstall the system."

Ashley had no idea what he was talking about, but he did have a nice voice.

"So you're kind of like the original Mr. FAQ," she said, "only without a clue."

"Exactly!" he smiled. "My dad, he's into answers. Me, I'm really big on questions. So…may I help you with any of your questions?"

Ashley scratched her head. "How do we get rid of pop-up ads?"

"Are you concerned about them?" He fired a question of his own right back.

"Well, are they supposed to keep popping up everywhere?"

"Would it be a problem for you if they did?"

Enough already!

"What about these sites?" Jessi pointed at the glowing yellow letters just below the surface of the floor.

"What about them?" he asked.

"I mean, are they safe? If we checked one of them out, could we get back?"

"Another good question. I like that one a lot. I don't know."

Oh, brother!

He beamed at them. "But I'll tell you what. If you wait right here, maybe I can find out for you."

One thing about FAQ Jr.: When he decided to leave, he didn't waste any time.

"Hey, wait!" Jessi tried to follow him, but she must not have looked down to see where she was going. She stepped smack on a link, fading for a moment before completely disappearing, leaving Ashley all alone.

Not for long though. Naturally Ashley would have to go after her. But what if Austin was looking for them from the Outside? How would he find them?

"A note," she mumbled to herself as she pulled out the mini-golf pencil from her pocket. The back of her wrinkled music competition program was blank, but she had to peek inside at the picture of the Yamaha Pro keyboard for just a moment.

How much time was left before it was her turn to sing? Was the contest already over?

Ashley sighed and glanced at the link Jessi had disappeared into; then she wrote in big letters: AUSTIN: WENT TO FANNY CROSBY LINK, *WWW.FANNYCROSBY HYMNS.COM.* BE RIGHT BACK. JESSI AND ASHLEY.

She laid down the program where Austin could see it, took one more look around, and jumped into the link.

Be cool, Austin told himself as Tucker Campbell came back down the hall. He thought he should probably type a little faster and without looking, like this: *lkjlkjs lkjslkjs lkjl kjss slkjs kljsj jlj lkjslkj slkjs...*

He could type 120 words a minute this way, and it must have looked impressive to anyone watching. Before Tucker plopped down beside him, Austin clicked back to the Web browser to surf the Internet.

"Have you found your sister yet?" She glanced at his screen. "I'm so worried about her. Even while I was singing, I could hardly concentrate."

"But you did okay?"

She flashed an ear-to-ear smile. Oh yes. She'd done okay.

"That's good."

"But Ashley? Is she coming back in time?"

He scratched his head, still not sure what had gone wrong. "I checked the *Musicpedia* site. It's just a lot of links. Ashley and Jessi aren't where I thought they would be."

"But how long?" Tucker wiped her eyes as if she might cry any minute. "How long do you think they're going to be gone?"

"I don't know. But look. This is where they were supposed

to be." He clicked back to *www.musicpedia.com*. "I mean,
is where I'm pretty sure they went. Do you see anything? T
might look like cartoon characters now, or they might blink
and off. You never know."

Tucker leaned closer to the screen. "Nothing weird.
girls. Just some trash someone left."

"Trash?" Austin took a closer look himself. "That shoul
be there. And it looks like there's some writing on it."

He could barely read the "Austin" and the "Be right ba
part, but it was enough to tell him who had written the no
As for the rest...

"The writing's too fuzzy." Austin rubbed his eyes. "W
do you think it says?"

Tucker took another look.

Finally she straightened up and smiled, "It says they w
to...uh...*www-dot-American-Shopping-Girl-dot-com* to
some shopping."

"No kidding?" Austin squinted once more. "You're s
that's what it says?"

"Absolutely, positively, 101 percent."

"You must have good eyes."

"Well..." She smiled. "Will that help you find them?"

"Maybe." Austin grinned and typed the new Web addr
into the browser. Now he'd be able to track them dov
"Thanks!"

"Didn't I tell you I'd be glad to help?" Tucker got to her feet and checked her watch with another winning smile. "I just hope you find them in time."

www.FannyCrosbyHymns.com

Who had turned out the lights?

Ashley wasn't sure what to expect at *www.FannyCrosby Hymns.com,* but she hadn't expected this. She waved her hand in front of her face and didn't see even a shadow. Very strange.

"Jessi?" She reached out for her aunt and felt her arm.

"Oh, there you are, Ash. I think FAQ Jr. got away."

"How can you tell when it's pitch-black?"

"Pitch-black? Open your eyes."

"They're open."

"And you can't see the parlor and the red-velvet wallpaper?"

"No. What are you talking about?"

"And the old piano over there by the window?"

"Jessi, I'm telling you, everything's dark. Totally dark."

"Maybe it'd help if you took off those grandma sunglasses."

"What?" Ashley felt the glasses on her face, though she had no idea where they had come from. Taking them off didn't change a thing.

"This is weird," she said. "Really weird."

"Yeah, but you do look really cute in that old-fashioned, frilly dress."

Ashley felt the lace trim on her sleeve and tried to figure out what had happened.

"This has never happened to me before. Maybe it's a glitch in the program."

"A glitch that makes you blind and dresses you up in a cool costume? How come I didn't get an outfit?"

"I have no idea, but I think we'd better go back. I sure don't want to stay this way for long."

"Oh, come on. We just got here, and this is my first visit to a true Web site. I wonder which one it is."

"That part's easy, *www-dot-FannyCrosbyHymns-dot-com*." Ashley remembered the name from her note to Austin.

"Fanny who? What kind of name is that?"

"Fanny Crosby. She lived back in the 1800s and wrote lots of hymns. Thousands of them."

"Oh"—Jessi sounded disappointed—"like organ music with lots of verses."

"Verses that meant something. And music that people liked. The thing is, she was…"

Ashley's voice trailed off. *Oh…* Weird as it was, she thought she understood what was going on now.

"She was what, Ash?"

"Blind." Ashley balanced the glasses back on her nose after poking herself with them. "Fanny Crosby was blind."

Ashley listened to the *tick-tock* of the parlor clock for a couple of seconds while she waited for Jessi to get it.

"That's it!" she chirped suddenly. "The old 1800s dress, the glasses, being blind… You didn't just drop in on the *Fanny Crosby* Web site, Ashley. You *are* Fanny Crosby."

Someone knocked just then, and Jessi yelped.

"Forty minutes," a man said. "Forty minutes until my train leaves. Can you do it, Fanny?"

"Wait a sec," said Jessi. "This is all going too fast for me."

Ashley paused before answering. Amazing how much you could figure out about a person even without seeing him. The man sure wanted something in an awful hurry. He sounded older, maybe middle-aged, and he had a deep, rich voice.

"Fanny?" he asked. "Are you all right? You look different. Sharper somehow."

Internet people often said that about internauts—real people like Ashley who traveled around the World Wide Web.

"Did you say Fanny?" Ashley cleared her throat. "That'd be me, I guess."

"Wait!" Jessi sounded worried, but Ashley held up her hand.

"It's okay." She turned to look toward where she guessed the man stood. "Now, what can I do for you?"

The man jumped right in. "I'll play my tune if you can offer some lyrics. The way we've done before?"

"Sure." Ashley was getting into the act. "Go for it."

She heard him stride over to the other side of the room; then she heard the scoot of a wooden chair or bench and the slow, steady playing of…

Hmm. Sounds familiar.

Still the man played on, and Ashley thought the melody sounded pretty catchy, with a bit of a bounce.

When he finished, he sat quietly as if waiting.

And waiting. Was something more supposed to happen?

"I'm still not sure how you do it, Fanny. If I had a memory for the Scriptures like yours, why…"

He didn't finish his thought, and all Ashley heard was the steady *tick-tock* of the clock.

"Hmm." Ashley wasn't sure she could do this. "So you want me to come up with the words, right here, right now? Just like that?"

"Well, if you don't know—"

"No, you're right. This is what Fanny Crosby was known for. I mean, that's what she's famous for, right?"

"And what words would you...er...Fanny, want to put with this tune?"

Ashley tried to think of something clever, but all that came to mind were the words of the song she'd memorized for the Greatest Young Vocalist Competition: *Love has got a hold of me, ooo-ooo...*

Oh no. Somehow she didn't think they would match his tune very well, so she tried noodling on some new lines.

"Okay, okay." At last she clapped her hands. "I think I've got something. What rhymes with heart?"

"Hay cart?" volunteered Jessi. "Kmart?"

"Pardon me?" Their visitor probably didn't have a clue what Jessi meant.

"Forget it." Ashley sighed. "I'm no good at this. I need to write down the words, look at them. Know what I mean?"

There was another pause from the man at the piano. "Perhaps another time."

"She didn't mean to mess up your song or anything," Jessi offered. "I think she needs more time to think it through. Give us a call later, and she'll have something great for you."

There was another pause, and Jessi fumbled for more

words. "Or…or stop by. Write us. People here write, don't they? Or maybe you could e-mail. E-mail, you know?"

This time the silence lasted so long Ashley got a little nervous. And the next time their guest spoke, Ashley could tell he was not a happy camper.

"What have you done with Fanny?" he demanded. Ashley felt the eyeglasses being pulled from her face.

She held up her hands. "I can explain everything."

"You're not Fanny." The man's voice rose. "I thought there was something strange the moment I saw you. You're…you're a Fanny impersonator!"

"W-we can explain," Jessi sputtered. "See, we dropped in by accident when—"

"Jessi!" Ashley turned toward the sound of her aunt's voice. "I don't think he cares about the details."

"I should say—"

"Anyway," Ashley continued, "we've stayed here long enough."

"But what about my song?" the man wanted to know. "And what about Fanny?"

"I think she'll be right back once we leave, sir." Ashley hoped she was right; she was guessing.

She leaned closer to Jessi. "Get us out of here!" she whispered. "Please!"

"How?"

"Find a link. On the floor. On the wall. Anywhere."

"I must insist that you return Miss Crosby at once!" By this time their guest was coming unglued.

"I'm really sorry." Ashley tried to apologize but didn't know what good it would do.

"Ooh, here's a cute link," said Jessi. "How about *www-dot-GreatConcertsOnline-dot-com*?"

"Fine." Ashley reached out to find Jessi's hand. "Just don't let go of me when you step on it."

"Maybe you could pick up some pointers at this link, Ash. Learn how to perform better and—"

"Sounds good." Ashley waved her hand blindly, still trying to find Jessi. *Bam!* She smacked someone in the nose.

"Ow!" cried the man.

"Sorry!" Ashley quickly turned away and latched on to an arm, hoping it was the right one.

CHAPTER 8

Un-American Shopping Girls

"I just don't get it. This can't be right." Austin quickly clicked through the *American Shopping Girl* site one more time, page after page after page. Tucker, taking another break from watching the competition, looked over his shoulder.

Ashley and Jessi sure had an awful lot of places to hide here. Buy the books here. Read a story there. Meet a character at another place. This site was mondo big. But ten minutes had passed, and he still hadn't found any trace of them.

And now his watch showed only about thirty minutes left before Ashley had to sing. Austin sighed and looked up at the ceiling for a second.

Hopeless.

"There!" Tucker pointed at the corner of the screen, and Austin nearly jerked his neck out of joint trying to see what she had spotted.

"Where?" He checked out the photo of a pioneer cabin. "I don't see anything."

Tucker paused, then frowned. "It looked like your sister. She waved at me. She's not there now though."

"Yeah, see, that doesn't make sense. Why would she wave? Usually from the inside it's hard to see what's going on out here, especially with a laptop or a flat screen because the screens are built differently. You have to get up really close."

"Maybe it was someone else." Tucker shrugged, and Austin kept clicking on the cabin to double-check.

Nothing.

"Even if it was Ashley, I don't understand why she and Jessi would have linked here to this site. They knew I would be looking for them. And I thought the *Musicpedia* portal site had only music links. How'd they end up here?"

"Have you been able to find them on a music link?"

"Not yet." *Obviously.* "I checked a few before coming here, but nothing so far."

"Well then."

Austin sighed. Maybe Tucker was right. Maybe he needed to ask somebody for help. Quick.

"Or maybe you just need to take a break." Tucker stretched. "Your brain will work better after a break. Mine always does when I'm doing homework late at night."

Yeah, he knew what she meant.

She wasn't finished. "Come listen to the rest of the contest I'm going to win," she said. "I mean, the contest I *or* your sister is going to win."

"I don't think so." Austin shook his head. "I have to keep looking for her."

After all, he explained, maybe the link hadn't worked right, and maybe they were stuck between two places. What then?

"I don't know about all that technical stuff," she told him. "But listen. You want to help them, right?"

Austin nodded.

"And you're not helping them now, are you?"

He shook his head no.

"Why not?"

He looked at Tucker. Was she being serious? "Because I can't find… I can't get to the right link… I can't think—"

"Exactly!" She snapped her fingers and pulled him to his feet. "You can't think. You need to be able to think. And if you're ever going to think, you have to give your mind a five-minute break. So you're coming with me to watch the next singer."

"But—"

"No buts. It's for your sister's good."

"Uh, I don't know about that."

As she started to pull Austin down the hallway, it was clear Tucker wasn't going to let him argue anymore.

"No, really." He planted his feet on the floor. "Thanks for trying to help. I really appreciate it. But I can't quit now."

Tucker opened her mouth as if to say something, and for just a second she squinted at him like he was a little crazy. But only for a second. Then she let go of his arm.

"Up to you." She smiled her biggest smile and headed back down the hall.

"AND NOW!"

Ashley found herself lined up with three other people on a round wooden platform ten feet down in a very odd pit. She squinted at the bright red and yellow lights swirling above them as an announcer shouted to a screaming crowd that must have been sitting somewhere above her.

How do you like that—from being blinded by darkness to being blinded by spotlights. And where was Jessi?

Everyone else onstage looked ready for the signal to begin as they held their wireless microphones. The guy to her left grinned and nodded, while the other guy and a girl on Ashley's right studied the floor, waiting, tapping their feet. All three looked maybe ten years older than Ashley.

And she wondered, *Do I look like them?*

Well, she was sure dressed like them, in a sparkly blue

blouse and jeans with a silver belt buckle that glinted in the lights. Her hair was swept back and springy, the way a pop singer might wear it.

"So"—she gripped her microphone the same way the others were—"looks like I'm in the group too."

The guy on her left must have heard her.

"This was what you wanted, wasn't it, kid?" He didn't look at her but kept his eyes fixed straight ahead, a stage smile pasted on his face. "You want to perform?"

"Sure."

"You want to be in front of people?"

"I think it would be fun."

"You want to sing?"

"I've been practicing."

"Well, now's your chance."

Maybe it was. The floor shook as it slowly raised them through a big hole in the stage floor. And as their elevator locked into position, the lights hit Ashley full in the face. That's when the crowd screamed even louder, nearly drowning out the announcer, who was yelling at the top of his voice: "AND NOW, THE ONLINE MOMENT YOU'VE BEEN WAITING FOR!"

Another big scream from the crowd. "WELCOME TO *WWW-DOT-GREATCONCERTSONLINE-DOT-COM.*"

Cool.

CHAPTER 9

ONLINE JAMMIN'

GreatConcertsOnline? Everything on this site—the stage, the singers, the audience—looked pretty real. Or almost real. Ashley could see a banner off to the left side of the stage hanging all the way from the ceiling to the floor with a list of things to click on. It looked the way someone would see it on a Web site. It listed a *Concert Schedule, Bios, Buy the CDs,* and a place to *Contact Us.* She could see tiny arrows clicking on the bars. People on the Outside were definitely visiting this place.

For now it looked as though she was stuck on the performance page. The audience was completely bonkers with excitement, as in scream-yourself-hoarse bonkers. The funny thing was, Ashley could hear one familiar voice above the rest of the crowd, chanting her name over and over, louder and louder.

"ASH-ley, ASH-ley, ASH-LEY!"

She had to smile as she spotted Jessi leaning over the rope railing in front of the stage, yelling her lungs out and waving both arms. As the fog machine cranked up, along with even more colored lights, Ashley almost forgot that Austin had to be wondering what had happened to them. But the lights pinned her down, and the music was coming up from behind. She heard a guitar, drums, a keyboard, and a bass.

And then she thought of something.

"Excuse me"—Ashley leaned over and tried to holler in the ear of the guy next to her. He tilted his perfect "do" toward her—"but do you know what we're supposed to be singing?"

He laughed as the backup musicians built up to their opening number—as in *nice joke*. With all the bright lights and fog and stuff, maybe he couldn't see she was an internaut. So she glanced to both sides and did what the other singers did.

They grabbed the microphones. Fine. She could do that. Next they leaned in and started *ooo*-ing in time to the music. Piece of cake so far. The swaying was no problem either. And then it was time to sing.

Five seconds in, the guy on her left started giving her panicked looks. Ashley was about two words behind the others, which made her sound like a really bad echo.

Then came their big mistake: They all swiveled to let her

take the solo. It seemed to Ashley that she'd had a nightmare like this once. She moved her lips but nothing came out. By this time not even the end of the song could save her.

She sighed with relief to see everything fade around her as someone clicked on the banner. *Thank you.* Someone Outside was coming to the rescue.

Sort of.

Because now, instead of wearing her pop-concert uniform, she'd been changed into the queen of a rodeo, complete with a white cowboy hat, pointed-toe, leather cowboy boots, jeans, and a belt with a big silver buckle. She heard a country steel guitar in the background, warming up.

Giddyap and yee-haw.

But no. Whoever was mousing around clicked on another option, and a moment later Ashley was standing on the stage of a gold-plated opera house. She looked down at her long, formal white gown. Too bad she didn't know how to sing in German. She looked for the exit, but a man in a Viking costume was blocking the way.

Click. Somebody was having a lot of fun playing performing-Barbie dress-up with Ashley. And this time the other three singers returned wearing red and white striped shirts and holding banjos. The boys wore handlebar mustaches, so Ashley felt above her lip, just to be sure. *Whew. That's a relief.*

But when they joined in their three-part harmony and

looked to her for the fourth part, Ashley just forced out the first note she could come up with.

The sour-lemon expressions on their faces told her all she needed to know.

And this was supposed to be cool?

Everybody in the audience was silent, blown away by what they'd heard.

"Well, I thought it was great." Jessi's voice echoed in the quiet-as-death concert hall as she turned to the people around her. "Really."

That's when the reviews started zinging at Ashley, online reviews from people Outside who had something to say. Their words looked as big as pianos as they flew in from the ceiling. When they hit the stage, they shattered into a million pieces, but not before the singers had a chance to read them and groan.

What's up with the new live performance? said one review. *That singer looked like a deer in the headlights. —J. L. from Dallas.*

Thanks for the kind words, J. L.

Ka-BASH! More words piled onto the stage, freight train–style.

Ashley remembered her mother telling her once that if she couldn't say something nice about someone, she shouldn't say anything at all. These reviews came from people whose mothers had not said that to them. Right after J. L.'s review came another from D. P. in Miami: *Some performers have off nights. This was off off. Minus three stars.*

D. P.'s jab made them all jump for cover, and all Ashley could do was apologize—not to the mean reviewers, but to the others in the group.

"I'm really sorry," she told them, ducking behind a tall speaker. "I didn't mean to spoil your concerts. I didn't even mean to come here. It was an accident. I thought it would be—"

She couldn't finish, and she wasn't sure if her apologies were doing any good. But when another review came zinging in, she felt a strong hand grab her by the back of the collar and pull her away from the stage with a funny *POP!*

CHAPTER 10

Web Lessons

Being backstage wasn't so bad. Ashley nearly tripped over all the old backdrops and rumpled costumes and props, but it was better than being in that spotlight.

"Uh-uh-uh." A man tapped Ashley on the shoulder with his conductor's baton. "You don't need to thank me for rescuing you from your bad reviews. You just listen to Ernie in your very own pop-up instructional window here at *www-dot-GreatConcertsOnline-dot-com,* and you'll be a professional musician in seven easy lessons, guaranteed."

"But—"

"Here we go. Hold your instrument like you mean it. Elbow bent. Bow ready."

Ashley looked around for help. She tapped on the button next to her foot. *Zzat!* Her instrument changed from a violin to...

Ernie smiled.

"The tuba?" he asked her. "Good choice. Let's first talk about breathing." He took a deep breath himself and started to let it out. "See? Breath control is everything. In fact—"

Zzat! She touched the link again just as Jessi came running around the corner.

"Whoa!" she puffed, skidding to a stop. "I thought your disappearing was part of the act. But then when the group kept singing without you, I—"

"Uh-uh-uh." Ernie brought his baton around like a sword. "We're in the middle of a saxophone lesson here, where expert musician Ernest J. Billings helps you master your instrument of choice in seven easy lessons. Click on the bottom of the page for payment options."

Jessi put up her hand. "I don't think—"

"I talk; you listen," he insisted. "Visa, MasterCard, or Discover cards gladly accepted. Now, let's talk about fingering, how you press the keys on your instrument."

Ashley gave her aunt a weak smile. She wasn't sure how they'd gotten themselves into this one—it seemed like a Web site within a Web site. As Alice in Wonderland would say, "Curiouser and curiouser."

In the distance they could hear the announcer once more.

"Sounds like they're starting the stage show again," whispered Ashley. "I think I'll pass this time."

"Oh, you should have seen it, Ashley," Jessi gushed. "From

the audience we could zoom in on any one of the singers, find out all about them, get the words to the songs. We could even click on live-performance clips from different shows. It was very cool."

"So that's why my costumes kept changing."

"Young ladies!" Ernie straightened his back and gave them a stern look. "Let's pay attention."

But as the music grew louder on the other side of the stage curtain, Ashley couldn't help walking toward it. Which wasn't too weird in itself, except her feet began to trip her. It felt as if she were walking on a tilted floor, sliding downhill.

"Where are you going?" asked Jessi.

Ashley had no idea what was happening, but the louder the music became, the stronger the pull—right toward the outside stage. Step by step, closer and closer she moved. A slide here, a shuffle there. As if her feet were deciding on their own what to do.

"This is too weird." The more Ashley tried to lean against the pull, the stronger it got, and the more she felt like a puppet.

Ernie puffed out his cheeks and shook his head.

"I'm sorry." Ashley slipped toward the exit. "I can't help it."

"Oh yes, you can." Ernie reached out to grab her hand. "When you sign up for seven lessons, you take all seven. No refunds!"

"AND NOW," boomed the announcer, "LIVE AND IN CONCERT, IT'S—"

Good thing Ernie had a strong grip. Plus Jessi grabbed Ashley's other hand just as Ashley's legs swung up to point compass needle–straight at the stage. Even so, Ashley could feel the tug of the stage as the crowd cheered.

"Don't let go of me!" she begged them as her fingers began slipping. *My life as a human bungee cord.* She'd once read a book with a title something like that.

"I...can't...hold...on," Jessi grunted. "Where's FAQ Jr. when you need him?"

The cyberbutler's son must have heard her because— *pop!*—he pushed his head in from between the stage's side curtains.

"Still checking on that question for you!"

"What"—Jessi gasped—"question was that?"

"Don't you remember? You asked how safe these music sites are. I'm still doing some research to find out."

And *pop!* he was off again.

"Research? Yeah, so are we. The hard way." Jessi clearly was losing the tug of war.

Ashley scanned the floor, her nose inches from doing a snowplow. Not knowing the words or the motions, she was headed for another nightmare performance. She tried to read some of the links in the floor as she slipped by. Unless—

"That one." Ashley tried to point with her nose. "Hit that link, Jessi! We need to get out of here."

Jessi stomped at the floor, but it was probably for the best that she missed the first one, *Click Here for More Musical Instruction.* Ernie had given them quite enough of that for now, thank you.

Speaking of her would-be music teacher, he was still pulling on Ashley's left arm for all he was worth. She appreciated that, even if he was just trying to hold on to her business.

"Keep your fingers limber when pressing the keys," he told her. "Use the fingertips, keeping the fingers bent just so."

"Thanks for the advice," she told him.

Jessi found another link in her stomp dance.

"Click Here for Music History Links," she read. "Gotcha!"

Ernie finally had to let go as their Web world faded to black.

CHAPTER 11

FoLLow the Links

🖱

"I need help." Austin took a deep breath and stared at his feet. How would he explain things so they didn't sound as unbelievable as they were? "Ashley and Jessi are lost inside the Internet, and I can't find them."

Whoosh! A toilet flushed, and Austin jumped as a little boy marched out of the stall behind him.

Phooey. He hadn't seen any feet below the doors when he'd stepped in here to practice what he was going to tell Mr. Hayward.

"Why can't you find them?" asked the blond-haired kid as he turned on the faucet to wash his hands.

Austin clutched his laptop and tried to look as if it were all a joke. "Never mind." He started to walk out, but the little boy wasn't through.

"My mom says to stay where we are if we get lost."

Austin nodded. "That's good."

"Or else we should go back to the first place everybody started from and wait there. Like when we went to The Field Museum in Chicago to see Sue the Dinosaur, and I got lost. I went right back to the front door, and my dad…"

The door swung shut behind Austin, who wondered, *Maybe the little guy is right. Go back to the beginning.* Going back to where the girls had started out was the one thing he still needed to do before he gave up. He'd visit the very first site one more time.

The little boy joined him out in the hall.

"Thanks, kid."

The boy grinned, and Austin trotted down the hallway to try again. With only about twenty minutes left, he'd try one more time before he asked for help. So forget *www-dot-American-Shopping-Girl-dot-com,* the place Tucker said she had seen Ashley. It was time to take another look at the *Music-pedia* site—and the note.

Austin scrolled through the portal site where he thought the girls had started out. The red site had dozens of links to music sites. Since he had already clicked on so many of them, though, it was hard to tell which ones had been visited and which ones had not.

"Come on. Where…"

There. The note! This time Austin didn't even try to squint to read the fine print. He simply copied and pasted it into a graphics program, what he should have done in the first place.

What had Tucker said? *They went to* www-dot-American-Shopping-Girl-dot-com *to do some shopping. Absolutely, positively, 101 percent.*

For the first time he wondered about what she'd said. And he wondered why it had taken him so long to wonder. Well, duh. Tucker Campbell had told him what to do, and he'd done it. Now he was going to see for himself what the note said.

Austin hit Sharpen to make the letters in the note clearer; then he clicked on the magnifying glass icon to make them bigger. A little clock spun around for a minute on the screen to tell him the computer was thinking, and then...

The picture of the note filled up his screen. "Austin," he read aloud. "Went to...Fanny Crosby link, *www.FannyCrosby Hymns.com.* Be right back. Jessi and Ashley."

Oh wow! So they hadn't gone to the *American Shopping Girl* site after all. And not to any of the other places he'd been searching either. Tucker had either been absolutely, positively, 101-percent wrong, or absolutely, positively, 101-percent lying.

He had a funny feeling that he knew which it was.

At least now Austin knew he had a better chance of tracking down the girls. He made up a quick to-do list as his fingers flew over the keyboard. To start, he clicked on the *Fanny*

Crosby site, careful not to disturb anything. He skimmed a couple of pages before he found a picture and the story of Fanny and her friend Howard Doane, and how they had once put together a song on the fly when he was on his way to a train station. It was called "Safe in the Arms of Jesus."

And there, right next to the picture, was a glowing red link, *www.GreatConcertsOnline.com*. On this site that red glow meant someone had visited the site. This was almost like following Hansel and Gretel's trail of breadcrumbs through the forest!

It turned out that *www.GreatConcertsOnline.com* had a bunch of different performances fans could click on to see, plus all kinds of info about their favorite singers and bands. Oh, and some kind of music-coach section where it looked like Ashley and Jessi had been too, but that seemed to be a dead end. Instead, Austin followed them through to *Music History Links,* where the trail went ice cold.

"Don't see any more links selected from here." He scratched his head. That would either mean he'd made some kind of mistake or Ashley and Jessi were very close. Maybe this was the end of the trail.

"Hey, guys!" he whispered at the computer. "You there?"

As he clicked through the *Music History* site he had come upon, he almost wished they weren't. He paused for a moment to study the part about the apostle Paul and his music.

Conditions in a Macedonian jail had to be horrible for Paul and his friend Silas, he read as he scrolled through. *Few people got out alive and well from the dark and damp cells.*

Austin kept reading, wondering what a cold, dark prison had to do with music.

CHAPTER 12

Not ALone?

Ashley huddled under a scrap of a blanket, shivering and miserable. She could feel the damp brick she was sitting on through the disgusting, scratchy robe made of rough cloth she was now wearing.

"Jessi?" She was afraid to raise her voice, afraid something would hear them in the dark. As far as she could tell, she was in a small room with the sound of water dripping all around her.

Worse than the darkness was the smell, a stink that made her stomach churn so badly she wished she didn't have to breathe. She knew she'd been in barns that smelled tons better. Ashley pinched her nose and tried to get comfortable, but as she shifted she noticed that cold, heavy metal clamps dug into her ankles. She flexed her legs and heard the *clink* of chains, probably attached to the wall behind her.

"Here," squeaked Jessi. Her voice was the first bit of good

news in this nightmare of a site. This was far worse than standing up on stage. "I think we made a wrong turn somewhere. This is no *Music History* link, unless we're going to hear the theme song to some horror flick."

"Maybe I'll have to sing it," Ashley answered quietly as she reached out to try to find Jessi in the dark. A little humor might help in a situation like this.

Right.

It didn't take long for Ashley to discover that she was the only one wearing a wool smock. Jessi still sported her jeans and T-shirt. And while Ashley was chained to the wall, Jessi wasn't. *Nice.*

"Wow!" Jessi placed her hand on Ashley's. "I don't understand why it's always you and not me. I'm sorry you keep getting all the lousy roles."

"I don't get it either. Maybe it has something to do with the way I got onto the Web this time."

"At least we're both here, right?"

"True, but since I'm the one in chains, you have a job to do."

"What's that?"

"Find us a way out. Quick."

But Jessi didn't budge.

"No way am I exploring this place alone! And besides, what if I did find something? How would that help you?"

But what were they going to do? Sit there whispering, listening to the water dripping and voices moaning off in the distance—and the…*creature* scurrying across the floor.

"What's that?" Jessi scooted between Ashley and the wall.

"Aaaaahh!" Someone hit the stone floor with a dull thud. A moment later that someone flashed a small light in their faces.

"Did someone ask another q-q-question?" He barely got his words out through his chattering teeth.

"Junior!" Jessi brightened up. "You're back."

But their FAQ remix shook his head in the dim light.

"Uh-uh. No. I'm terribly sorry," he stammered, "but I don't do prison visits. We'll find another place to meet."

"But what about our questions?" asked Jessi.

"They're terrific. Insightful. Wonderful. But please don't ask any more for a while, okay?"

And with that he stumbled off into the dark.

"How do you like that?" Ashley couldn't believe it. "What was he, scared of rats or what?"

"Did you say r-r-rats?"

Ashley hadn't meant to scare her…just the opposite. But her words hadn't helped. She knew for a fact that if Jessi could have climbed up on her shoulders, she would have.

Anyway, the good news was that Ashley's eyes were slowly getting used to the dark. And the bad news was that Ashley's eyes were slowly getting used to the dark. She had started to make out a shape, a lump of darkness in the opposite corner. And she noticed a wheezing sound, barely more than a breath.

Jessi must have heard it too, judging from the way she dug her fingernails into Ashley's arm.

"Ashley?" Jessi's voice was soft but filled with quiet panic. "Tell me there's nobody else in this jail cell."

"Jessi, there's nobody else in this jail cell."

"That doesn't count. You didn't mean it."

Whoever it was sure didn't sound like FAQ Jr.

Ashley strained to see, but the shadow was too hard to make out. She decided to clear her throat and speak to it. If a monster was going to jump them, they would at least see it coming, right?

The dark thing in the corner moved.

Jessi's scream told Ashley she must have seen it too.

"Oh dear." Ashley rubbed the ear closest to Jessi, the ear that would now be deaf for the rest of her life. "Warn me next time you're going to do that, okay?"

And then the shadow rose to its feet with a clanking of chains.

Ashley put up her hands, karate-style, as if that would scare it off.

"Don't move!" she yelled. "I've got a black belt." *Sure I do.*

Somewhere back home in my closet, hanging up next to my brown belt and blue belt.

"Yeah!" whimpered Jessi. "So don't move."

They had expected a growl or a snarl—anything but a chuckle.

"I'm sorry to startle you," came a deep voice. "It's just that when I dozed off, Silas was sitting right where you are, with his ankles in chains. And now that I'm awake, it appears you are not Silas."

By this time Ashley could pick out a man's shape leaning against the far wall. As far as she could tell, he wore the same chains she did.

"Ashley and Jessi, is it?" he asked in a gentle voice.

Ashley gasped. How did he know?

He must have guessed her question. "I heard you talking to each other just now," he explained. "I'm no fortune-teller, though the girl Silas and I helped in the town square certainly was. Perhaps you know the story."

A small arrow clicked on their cellmate, and a pop-up window gave the details: *The apostle Paul and his traveling companion, Silas, were thrown into a Philippian jail after they cast out a demon in a slave girl. When the girl was no longer able to earn money for her owner by telling fortunes, he accused Paul of "throwing our city into an uproar by advocating customs unlawful for us Romans to accept or practice." The account is related in Acts 16.*

The words seemed to brighten their dark cell, but they glowed only for a moment before fading once again. Ashley sighed. This time, though, a sliver of light worked its way through a small hole in the door, shedding just enough brightness to show the man's beard and bald dome. He couldn't have been any taller than Ashley herself.

He spoke again. "So you know who I am supposed to be. But perhaps you can tell me what *you're* doing here, my internaut friends."

He knows, thought Ashley. *Are we that obvious?*

Even in the dark they must have looked a lot sharper than everything around them.

"It's my fault," Jessi tried to explain. "Ashley didn't want to come here, but I thought we should check out all the music sites we could so she could pick up a few tips and win the keyboard."

"Despite the fact that I am programmed to speak English," he told them, "I have no idea what you were just talking about. I assume, however, that you are musicians?"

Ashley: "Not really."

Jessi: "She is. Not me."

Paul: "I see. Well, we have an audience here."

Ashley and Jessi listened, and in the distance, maybe from down the hall, they began to hear faint voices, soft at first but growing louder.

A shiver ran up Ashley's spine.

The voices moaned, insisting on something Ashley could not quite make out. They called Paul's name, begging him...

For what?

CHAPTER 13

JaiLhouse Rock

"Getting closer…" Or so Austin hoped as he clicked through the pages of *www.musichistory.net*.

The site was actually kind of interesting. He slowed down to check out a page showing two men with chains clamped to their ankles—the apostle Paul and his buddy Silas—singing hymns in a Macedonian jail. The page was pretty dark, though, which made it hard to tell what either man looked like.

What did they do to get thrown into jail? Austin wondered. *Nothing!*

He started to read the story but knew he'd better get back to the search. Only fifteen minutes left before Ashley's show time! From what he could tell, Ashley had to be here somewhere. But where?

Click Here to Hear an Early Hymn?

Cool, but probably not. Instead he clicked over to a FAQ section where people could ask questions and get answers from the college professor of musicology who ran the site. Austin knew he didn't want to fire off an e-mail to just anybody, but he thought this one might be worth the risk.

"If Ashley and Jessi are stuck on this site"—he scratched his head and stared at the screen—"maybe they can get an e-mail."

And if they could get an e-mail, he could tell them how to get home. He started to type.

"Another song!" This time the prisoners grew bolder, shouting and banging on the inside of the thick, wooden doors of their cells. "Please! You must!"

For a moment Ashley had the sinking feeling she had landed in the middle of weird performance number three. Just as bad, each performance took Jessi and her farther and farther away from where they had started—and from where Austin had said he'd look for them. Who knew if the competition was already over and Tucker had won the keyboard?

The prisoners didn't care about her worries. They just upped the noise, yelling and banging on their doors, probably with their wooden eating spoons.

"What do they want?" asked Jessi, still crouched behind Ashley.

"You hear them," answered Paul. But when an outside door creaked open, the prisoners instantly fell silent. No one needed to explain to them who had just stepped inside the prison.

"The jailer," whispered the girls' cellmate.

Naturally the jailer demanded to know what all the noise was about. Ashley couldn't make out the whimpering answer from another prisoner...only the jailer's reply.

"Oh, he is, eh?"

Footsteps echoed outside in the hallway, and they were coming closer.

"He's coming this way," whispered Jessi, her hands gripping Ashley's shoulders.

Two weak shafts of lamplight flickered in from below and above the door, and Ashley couldn't help leaning over as far as her chains allowed to see what she could. There! A crack in the door gave her a peephole to the outside, where the jailer stood with a small oil lamp.

"See anything?" asked Jessi, but Ashley held up her hand. "Shh."

The jailer didn't move; he just stood outside the door as if waiting to burst in at any moment.

And Paul picked that time to start singing.

"He's still out there!" Ashley warned, but Paul must have known. Ashley held her breath and waited for the worst.

Nothing happened. Paul's voice sounded lonely as he sang the first verse of a slow Jewish song.

"List my tears on your scroll," he sang to a strangely beautiful tune.

The words sounded kind of like the words of a psalm Ashley had once memorized. These words had wings to fly up and out of their cell for everyone to hear. And now she knew what the other prisoners had been begging for—and why even the jailer had stopped to listen.

"Then my enemies will turn back"—Paul continued in his clear, low voice—"when I call for help."

He paused for a moment to let the song echo in their cell, and Ashley knew that angels could not have performed a more wonderful concert. Not because Paul had a special voice—he sounded pretty ordinary—but because the music itself was far from ordinary.

Paul pointed at her. "You'll sing along now, Miss Ashley? Silas sang with me before. Perhaps this is why you are here."

"Oh no." Ashley began to shake her head, thinking back to the onstage disaster they'd just escaped. But—and this was the surprising part—just as her feet had pulled her toward the stage at the pop concert, this time her *lips* seemed to form the words as he sang. Maybe she had memorized them once, back in youth group or Sunday school. Because when Ashley finally opened her mouth to sing, she knew the words.

"By this I will know that God is for me. In God, whose word I praise, in the LORD, whose word I praise—in God I trust; I will not be afraid. What can man do to me?"

For the next hour, maybe two, Ashley and Paul sang psalm songs together. He knew dozens of them, each with a different tune. Ashley would sing along, usually starting at the second verse and singing through to the end.

"How do you know all these songs?" Jessi asked.

Ashley wondered the same thing. And she wondered how long they could stay there, singing and listening to Paul in this prison that no longer seemed so horrible. Part of her didn't want to leave—it was definitely better than being back on stage. Even the audience was much better than any she could ever hope for. Sure, the prisoners and the jailer were listening, and Jessi, too. But it seemed to Ashley as if they were really putting on their little concert for an audience of One. For God.

She wasn't sure she could have explained to anybody what she was feeling, but that was okay. She didn't have to. And even though she knew no one was giving out Yamaha keyboards as prizes here, that didn't matter. She sang and sang until she couldn't hold her eyelids open any longer. Jessi even began to hum along. Was it midnight now? Later?

Ashley felt a hand on her shoulder, shaking her awake.

"Ashley?" Jessi whispered in her ear. "Don't you think we

should be leaving? The jailer's gone now. Paul will understand. It's been a couple of hours."

She nodded and rubbed the sleep from her eyes. So many things were hard to understand about the Internet, and time was one of them. Her watch still read 11:05, though she didn't know how that was possible. But one thing she did know: Her parents were going to be calling out the Illinois National Guard if she and Jessi didn't find their way back to Normal very soon.

"Okay, just find us a link." The singing had been nice, but Ashley would be glad to get out of her chains. If Jessi could find something close by and reach back to touch her, maybe that would work. "There should be one around here some…"

Her voice trailed off when the floor began to shake beneath them. Harder and harder, like a bad cough that wouldn't stop. Ashley felt sandwiched between the deadly shiver of the earth and the groaning mass of the building above them. Chunks of plaster and rock cracked off the ceiling as the heavy door splintered and fell, nearly crushing her feet.

It could be that Ashley had given her last concert.

CHAPTER 14

Virtual Rumble

"Austin Webster!" Austin and Ashley's mom could sound pretty serious when she wanted to. As she charged down the hall toward him, Austin knew there was no escape. "Do you know what time it is?"

He checked his watch.

"Uh, 11:06?"

His mom planted herself in front of where he sat in the hallway and looked down at him.

"Your sister was supposed to meet us for warmups in the cafeteria fifteen minutes ago, but nobody seems to know what's happened to her. You haven't seen her?"

"Wish I had, Mom." He scratched his head and did his best to look calm.

"Her friend Tucker told me she had seen her in the halls with Jessi, but that was awhile ago."

Her "friend" Tucker? Right.

"Tucker's probably right." But he didn't explain what the "friend" had done to try to make sure Ashley lost her chance to compete. "I think she's with Jessi."

His mom waited for more. "That's all you can tell me?"

"I've been looking all over for her."

"So that's what you're doing sitting there right now? All right. But she's going to miss everything she's been working so hard for. I just don't understand it."

"I don't either, Mom, but look." Austin pointed at his laptop screen. "From right here I can get into any security camera in the school. See?"

He clicked out of the music-history Web site and showed her a half-dozen black-and-white shots of the school hallways. They were taken every few seconds by a security camera. "Here's the office. Here's the hallway in front of the gym. Here's the—"

"All right." She straightened up. "I have no idea how you do all that or even if—"

"Don't worry. Mr. Hayward is fine with it," Austin assured her. "In fact, he thinks it's great."

The look on his Mom's face asked, "Are you sure?"

That's when his laptop screamed. Or rather, someone inside it screamed. Someone who sounded an awful lot like Aunt Jessica. He slammed the screen down, but Austin's mom stiffened.

"What was that?" she asked.

"Not sure. But I'll find out."

"One of your video games?"

Austin thought it would have been nice if that were all it was.

"I'll let you know as soon as Ashley turns up," he promised. He intended to do all he could to keep that promise. "I'll…keep looking for them."

Finally she nodded and turned to go.

Austin sighed with relief when the hallway door clanged shut behind her, and he reopened his laptop to the dark view of Paul and Silas in prison, the last place the girls' trail had led him. But if they were there, why hadn't Ashley shown herself?

And what in the world was that scream all about?

Back in the dot-com prison, Ashley was doing her best to keep Jessi from losing it completely. Which was pretty tough, seeing as how their cell had just crumbled around them.

"It's okay!" she told Jessi, brushing the dust from her aunt's hair. "You know the story. Paul and Silas survive the earthquake."

"But we're not Paul or Silas, are we?"

"We're Silas, okay? Or close enough. Now hang in here with me."

Easy for her to say, but with the doors broken and at least a dozen other prisoners crowding into what was left of their cell, well…

"This is our chance!" yelled one of the men. "I say we make a run for it before the jailer wakes up or comes back."

"No!" Paul would have none of it. "Everyone stays here."

"But your chains are loose," argued a burly guy in his twenties. "Take your friends and leave while you still can."

"I said no. God still has something for us here."

"We like your singing, Paul of Tarsus," another prisoner piped up, "but you're crazy."

"He is not!" Jessi jumped to his defense. "He's a really nice guy for an Internet character."

"Thank you," said Paul. "I think."

"Shh!" warned a lookout who had been watching the street. "The jailer's coming."

Too late. Several of the men shrank back to the wall.

"We should have run when we had the chance," mumbled the man who had argued with Paul.

Ashley heard the jailer stop in the hallway, breathing hard.

"No!" he cried. She peeked out around their half-broken

cell door to see him leaning against what was left of the door frame. "They're all gone."

He probably said that because he saw that the other cell doors had also broken open. Who wouldn't assume that everyone who could leave had left the damaged jail? Ashley caught her breath when she saw the glint of the jailer's sword. She turned to warn the others, but Paul wasted no time stepping out into the jailer's flickering torchlight.

"We're all here, sir. Don't hurt yourself."

A pause…then, "All of you?"

"You heard the man." Jessi had the nerve to back up Paul. "A dozen smelly guys and two girls, all stuffed into this lousy hole. Who can we complain to about this dump?"

"Jessi!" Ashley still had her eye on the jailer's sword.

"Internauts." Paul sighed and shook his head. "Sorry about that."

By now the rest of the prisoners had come out of their hiding places, and three more Roman soldiers had arrived to help the jailer. Even with the earthquake damage, there had been only one way out of the jail. The soldiers' torches lighted up the prison as they led the prisoners back to their places.

"You had plenty of time to run after the earthquake," the jailer told them. His hands shook as he fell trembling before Paul, Ashley, and Jessi. "Why didn't you?"

"As I was telling the men…" Paul glanced over at Ashley.

"Er…sorry—*and* the girls—we didn't leave because God has plans for us…and for you, friend. Please get up."

The jailer looked pale in the torchlight. Ashley remembered looking that way once last winter when a rotten flu bug was going around.

"I listened to you singing," the guard replied, now standing but still shaking all over. "But…but you all could have been free if you'd wanted."

"We already are." Paul smiled, and the jailer sighed and closed his eyes.

"Then tell me," he said, his voice shaky and quiet, too quiet for the soldiers to hear. "Tell me about this freedom you have. Tell me what I have to do."

Paul smiled as if he knew the answer to a secret he'd been hoping to share. He glanced over at the girls.

"Do you want to tell him," he asked Ashley, "or shall I?"

CHAPTER 15

DIGITAL PLUNGE

Never mind that it must have been three in the morning Macedonia time. Ashley couldn't wipe the huge smile off her face as she raced back up the rocky trail to the city. One of the jailer's young daughters, her dark hair glistening in the moonlight, held on to her hand. She must have been five or six.

"You've been baptized like that too?" the girl asked.

"Well, yeah." Ashley paused, wanting to say the right thing. "Only not in a river like you, and not with my whole family. I have to say your baptism was pretty cool."

"Not too cool." The little girl rubbed a rough cloth on her head. "I feel warm all over."

Ashley laughed as Paul began once more to apologize. "Not a regulation *mikvah*," he told them. "But even our Lord was baptized in a stream such as yours, so you're in good company."

"What's a mikvah?" Jessi asked Ashley, her voice low.

"A Jewish baptismal pool." Paul must have overheard the question.

Austin would have known that. He should have been there. But Ashley tried not to think too much of her brother and of home as they picked their way back through the quake-damaged city gates to the jailer's stucco home. Paul and Ashley and Jessi crowded with the jailer and his wife and their four young children into the family's main living room.

"And now you will all stay for breakfast, yes?" The jailer raised his hands to welcome them, and Ashley knew they couldn't say no. His wife began to bring in food and cups for them, setting everything on a long, low table off to one side. Jessi followed her, as if looking for a way to help.

"Drinking water," she said. "That I can do."

She must have found a bucket in the kitchen because a minute later she was lugging it back into the room, sloshing water all over the tile floor with every step.

"Hey, if you guys were Presbyterians, we could have done the whole ceremony right here."

"Jessi!" Ashley hurried over to help grab the handle, noticing as she did the links in the corner on the floor. Could be they were near the edge of this site. As Ashley reached out, Jessi stepped right in a puddle, sending her—and the bucket—flying.

"Whoa!" she yelled, trying her best to keep her balance.

Though Ashley saw it coming, she didn't know what to do about it. The bucket and water landed squarely on a link, and Jessi reached out to grab the bucket...just as it blinked and started to disappear. Ashley tried to hold her aunt back, but it was no use. She was sucked in along with Jessi and the bucket and a spilled gallon of cold water.

Ashley did manage to look over her shoulder as they hyperlinked out of there.

Paul was waving.

Austin looked at his watch for the tenth time in almost as many minutes. It was 11:15. Fifteen minutes to go before the program was done and the judges made their final decision. Ashley was supposed to go on stage in ten minutes or less. And if she didn't show, well, after hearing Tucker sing, everyone pretty much knew who would win the keyboard.

To make things worse, at any minute his mom might come charging back down the hall wanting to know what was *really* going on here.

The truth: He'd lost Ashley again, and there was no way he could explain that to their mom. He bit his lip, sure now what he had to do. So far his rescue from this side of the Internet hadn't done diddly.

The plan: He'd start from the Web site Ashley and Jessi had last been to, *www.musichistory.net,* and take an up-close look at the prison where Paul and Silas had sung hymns in the middle of the night. Could he get any closer to where the girls had been? And could he get them back in time?

One thing he did know was that he wasn't going to have any luck staring at the screen of his laptop. He had to dig deeper, go there himself. Besides, when he found them, he could show them how to get back. Or at least he thought he could.

He heard the footsteps of someone coming down the hallway. Probably Tucker coming to tell him that if his sister didn't show up really soon, the competition was all over.

Balancing the camera on a chair, he checked the viewfinder, made a few more adjustments, then hit the timer and hurried around to sit on the floor. *Whoops!* He couldn't forget his trusty laptop.

"Austin?" Tucker called from just around the corner.

He grabbed for his computer, still attached to the camera. Three...two...one...

Flash!

Ka-BOOOM! Austin hadn't remembered the Internet being so noisy last time. But his entry must have been pretty flashy, like fireworks on the Fourth of July. That's what it smelled like too. When he got over the tingling electric feeling that came from traveling the World Wide Web, a cloud of nose-curling sulfur smoke nearly gagged him.

Flash! *Ka-BOOM!*

Austin held up his hand to keep from getting hit by whatever was exploding in his face.

"Shall we continue firing, sir?" yelled a man through the smoke.

Austin coughed and tried to figure out what was going on. In the flashes of explosion after explosion, he could see he was standing on a wooden deck, like that of an old sailing ship. And he was wearing a funny uniform with a heavy, blue officer's overcoat that hung down to the back of knees, a white vest, tight white pants, and tall white socks. What was up with this? Maybe he shouldn't have messed with the camera settings quite so much. On his head perched a three-cornered hat like the kind George Washington had worn.

Only Austin had a feeling he wasn't the father of his country.

"Captain?" came the voice. "You signaled to cease firing?"

Austin had no idea where he had come in for a landing, except these folks sounded very British. This was obviously not the site he thought he'd programmed for. And what was up with the "captain" stuff? Better to play along now and find out later.

"No." His voice came out mousy and unsure. *Oh well.* He

cleared his throat and gave it his best British accent. "I mean, go ahead. Please proceed. Whatever."

The flashes and *ka-BOOMs* started up again, so Austin tucked his laptop inside his overcoat and stood with his fingers in his ears, wondering what was going on.

He inched toward the ship's railing, doing his best to see into the soft, pink light coming up on the distant shore. *Is it dawn?* At least his heavy wool uniform kept him warm. He could see the men around him focused on their jobs and on the fort in the distance. A man in the rigging of the ship yelled down at them.

"The American flag, sir!" the sailor hollered so everyone could hear. "It's still there."

"Great!" Austin replied. "I mean, what?" And then it dawned on him where he was. The British officer's suit suddenly felt unbearably hot and itchy. Now he could make out some of the warships around him, plus another smaller vessel stuck in between. Austin lowered his head, wondering how he'd escape the War of 1812.

And where were Ashley and Jessi?

CHAPTER 16

Rockets' Red BLare

⌂

Ashley coughed and gagged as she tried her best to catch her breath, but it was as if someone was spraying her straight on with a garden hose. Only this wasn't at all like the fresh water Jessi had spilled back at the jailer's home.

"I *hate* salt water," sputtered Jessi.

It seemed they were up to their elbows in waves or explosions. A zinging, whistling sound came at them from behind, louder and louder and…

Ker-SPLASH!

"That was—*hack-hack*—close!" Ashley couldn't stop coughing. But when she paused long enough to look around, she saw the stone walls of a fort in the light of dawn. It was full of holes from all the bombs bursting in the air and the cannonballs zinging around, exploding into bricks and water—but what wouldn't be?

"Where in the world are we *now?*"

"I have no idea," yelled Jessi. They held tightly to each other in the rockets' red glare, as more cannonballs came zinging in one after the other. Above them they could make out the broad stripes and bright stars of a huge, ragged-edged American flag flying from a tall flagpole.

It occurred to Ashley that this Web site looked a little different from the others she had visited. On the left she could make out a list of what was on the site, reading from top to bottom in big letters: *Home, Meet Mr. Key, Story of the Song, The Melody, FAQ,* and—*ker-SPLASH!*—something else she couldn't read.

Well, actually, the list was fairly standard for a Web site. But there on the right was something that looked like a thermometer with the words Zoom In at the top and Zoom Out at the bottom.

"Can you reach any of the links?" she asked Jessi, still keeping her head low. Another volley of cannonballs whistled in as Jessi shook her head no.

"Okay, how about the Zoom thingie?" She reached for it herself as she asked, then connected—just barely—with a handle. Jessi grabbed it too, and they both tugged as hard as they could.

"Zoom out!" yelled Jessi. That sounded fine to Ashley,

except that when they flew backward, their landing on a splintery wooden deck of a ship wasn't as smooth as they might have liked.

"Mercy!" A man in a dark coat nearly jumped over the side of the sailing ship when he saw them.

"Sorry to scare you like that." Ashley rubbed her head and tried to figure out where they'd landed. At least this was better than being in the line of fire. All around them ships flying British flags were still aiming their cannons at the shore. *Ka-BOOOM!* The little ship they were on, though, flew an American flag like the one flying over the fort, only it was much smaller.

"Cool Ben Franklin suit." Jessi was looking Ashley over.

"You know Dr. Franklin?" asked the man, eyes wide.

"Oh no, not—*hack-hack*—at all," Ashley tried to explain, as if she knew what she was talking about. "It's just that Jessi here, she's…"

Jessi was still wearing her Chiddix Chargers T-shirt, which wasn't looking too great anymore.

"I'm kind of cold, actually." Jessi broke in.

"Dr. William Beanes," said the man, nodding politely. "And you both must get out of the cold."

He took off his overcoat and placed it around Jessi's shoulders, which seemed like a gentlemanly thing to do. Ashley made do with her old-fashioned breeches and fancy button-down white shirt.

"We're—*hack-hack*—fine." But Ashley still was having trouble breathing. "And we're sorry to drop in like this."

"Not your fault, I'm sure." The doctor waved it off. "It appears the programming for this site has suddenly been changed. You're wearing Francis's clothing, but you're obviously not Francis."

"No, she's Ashley," Jessi jumped in. "And I'm Jessi. Who's Francis?"

"Francis Key, of course," he answered, as if they should have known. "He's been a friend of my family for years. He arranged for my release from the British invasion force, but until this is over, we're still being held prisoners here in the harbor, forced to watch the bombardment from our ship."

"You can't sail away from these guys?" Jessi pointed at the warships around them, but the answer was obvious. Not a chance.

"So this is..." Ashley turned to see, but she already knew.

"Baltimore Harbor." He pointed toward the horizon, where the flag flew against the growing light. "And that, I'm afraid, is Fort McHenry, still under attack."

Ashley nodded. "It's 1814"—this one she knew—"and I'm

supposed to be Francis Scott Key, the writer of 'The Star-Spangled Banner.' "

"Too cool!" Jessi looked as if she was warming up under Dr. Beanes's coat. "Ashley gets to write the national anthem. 'And the rockets' red blare' and all that, huh?"

"Oh dear." Dr. Beanes obviously wasn't keen on Jessi's version of the anthem. "I can see we shall need to expedite your departure before more damage is done."

"Expedite is good?" Jessi asked, clueless as ever.

He smiled as he led them to a glowing spot at the rear deck of the ship.

"He means he needs to get us out of here in a hurry," Ashley whispered. "We're in the way."

"My apologies," he told them, "but this is the only way I know of back to the Outside. Bon voyage."

Ashley looked down at the deck to see the faint red glow of *The Anthem in Sports*.

"Wait a minute!" cried Jessi. It seemed she was only just catching on as the War of 1812 faded from view. "Don't you want your coat back?"

CHAPTER 17

Virtual Wrigley

"FRESH ROASTED PEANUTS!" squawked a man as he stepped in front of Ashley and Jessi. "GET YER PEANUTS HERE!"

"I'll have some." Jessi tried to order, but Ashley grabbed her arm.

"No time for that."

"What? I'm hungry. With all this skipping around the Web, a girl has to eat something to give her energy."

"Fine, but how are you going to pay for them?"

"Hmm." Jessi's face fell as she realized what Ashley meant, but she perked up again when she looked around.

"Hey, someplace we know! Wrigley Field! And you're sure dressed up for a baseball game."

Sure enough, the Chicago Cubs were down on the field warming up, hitting a few balls. Their uniforms seemed a little loose and oversized though. And their gloves looked funny.

Ashley noticed she looked a little funny too—pretty fancy in a forties-style blouse and skirt and an old-fashioned hat decorated with tiny baby's-breath flowers dangling over the brim. Ashley perched the hat back on her head, wondering if the person she was dressed like now had spent hours gussying up for the party.

"Smashing!" One of the British ship's officers pushed in closer for a look at Austin's laptop. "We never get to see anything else on the Internet. It's just the bombardment of Fort McHenry, the War of 1812, and all that rot."

"Over and over and over…" moaned a sailor, leaning in to see for himself. "Horridly dull. One would think they'd grant us a change of jobs once in a while. Even Leftenant Brumbley here's ready for a change."

"So you can see outside our site on that piece of equipment?" asked another sailor.

"Sure. You can see just about anything, learn anything, visit anywhere, even buy things. That's the Internet."

"Fascinating." Leftenant Brumbley's jaw dropped. "You don't suppose you could show us—"

"Actually"—Austin hated to interrupt, but if he didn't watch it, he was about to become a Web guide—"I'm trying to find my sister and Jessi. If they're not here on this music-history site…"

He checked the search engine, looking for links to *www.musichistory.net*.

"Women?" asked one of the sailors.

"Uh…I guess. Looks like I just missed 'em."

He checked out a couple more links. *Early American Instruments?* No. *Pioneer Music?* Uh-uh. *The Anthem in Sports?*

"Hot dog!" He zeroed in on the link. Maybe this was it.

His audience looked at him and then back down at the screen.

"Looks like they may have hyperlinked to a Cubs game at Wrigley Field," he explained. "In 1942."

"Cubs?" asked a sailor.

Austin nodded and clicked through the site. "Soon as I see any sign of them, that's where I'm going too."

"We're viewing something that happens 128 years after the time of our site." The leftenant shook his head. "Incredible."

"I guess so…if you look at it that way. For me 1942 is sixty-some years back, even though the Internet doesn't really take anyone back in time. But look, if my sister's there, we should be able to spot her. She'll be really sharp and clear compared to other people."

"Hmm." Leftenant Brumbley leaned in even more. "It seems they're playing a strange form of cricket."

"Baseball, not cricket."

Cricket was an old English game played with two bases, a flat bat, and a ball. Maybe it was the great-great-grandfather of baseball, but it wasn't the same game. Austin zoomed in and out on the field and the stands. He clicked on the stats of the players, just to make sure Ashley wasn't in a Chicago Cubs uniform. You never knew.

There was Hiram "Hi" Bithorn, the first Puerto Rican to play in the big leagues and a rookie pitcher with the 1942 Cubs. If he'd had time, Austin could have clicked to learn about the baseball stadium in San Juan, Puerto Rico, that was named after Bithorn.

So what about Jimmie Foxx? Or Claude Passeau, the only Cub to make that year's all-star team? Nope.

Still no Ashley.

Well, then, how about this? Austin wondered as he clicked on the flag flying over an old black-and-white photo. A pop-up window explained how people really got into singing the national anthem that summer after World War II started.

" 'The Star-Spangled Banner' was first performed at a baseball game during the 1918 World Series," he read from his screen. "But the anthem wasn't played regularly until the start of World War II in 1939, and then through the 1940s."

"Oh dear." Leftenant Brumbley looked concerned. "We aren't still fighting each other in the 1940s, are we?"

"Oh no," Austin assured him. "We were on the same side that time. The British and Americans are great friends."

"Go, Yanks!" yelled one of the sailors.

"No, the Yankees are American League," Austin explained. "Cubs are National League. They don't usually play each other except... Oh, forget it."

"I see." The sailor nodded as if he understood. Then he leaned in and pointed. "What did you say your sister looks like?"

"You ready, miss?" A man in a hat shoved a big microphone on a stand in front of Ashley. "You're on in two."

He tapped the mike and gave her a thumbs-up.

She glanced around to see if there might be some mistake.

"You're on," Jessi whispered. "A solo. Isn't this what you always wanted?"

Was it? Not since the nightmare at *www.GreatConcerts Online.com.* And definitely not since the midnight concert in the Philippian jail. Ashley'd learned to sing for a greater audience there. Still, everybody here was waiting for her to sing. How could she not?

So Ashley opened her mouth, but only a hoarse whisper came out. Hardly the kind of voice she would need to sing the national anthem in front of thousands of people.

But it was way too late to run now. The men down
the field removed their hats as the announcer's voice echoe
through the stadium.

"And now, ladies and gentlemen, please join us in t
singing of our national anthem."

As the echo faded to a hush, every one of the 38,39
people in the crowd stood and waited to hear the first famili
words. Even the hot-dog and peanut sellers were quiet.

Ashley leaned close to the microphone, took a de
breath, and...

Her mind went totally blank. She had sung this song hu
dreds of times before, had dreamed of everyone looking
her, and had even rehearsed in her bedroom, holding a hai
brush microphone.

But now?

CHAPTER 18

Grand Slam

"Oh no!" Austin searched the deck of the ship one more time, but it was no use. "I thought there was going to be a link close by."

What now? He and the crew watched Ashley on the screen, plain as day. They'd even spotted Jessi, who was turning red in the face as she waited for Ashley to begin. No matter what it took this time, Austin wasn't going to let the girls get away. He hadn't come all this way for nothing.

He thought for a moment. Maybe he could save what he was seeing to his hard drive, kind of like recording a favorite TV show on a VCR. If he had time, he could probably reprogram them to another site. But what good would that do?

"Poor lass has forgotten it, has she?" Leftenant Brumbley shook his head.

"Come on, come on." Austin kept his eyes on the screen as a green light blinked in the corner. It was finally recording.

He saw Jessi quickly step up and hand Ashley a rolled-up piece of paper. Ashley glanced down at the paper, took another breath, and faced the microphone again. This time she launched right in.

"Say." A sailor stood up. "I know that tune! But the words are all wrong."

Well, the words might have been all wrong for the old English song, but they were all right for the crowd at Wrigley Field.

"Blest with victory and peace, may the heaven-rescued land
Praise the Power that hath made and preserved us a nation!"

It was "The Star-Spangled Banner" all right, only not the first stanza, the one everybody knows—Austin knew the song had more than one stanza.

With bright eyes and a glow on her face, Ashley sang the words as if she meant them. Austin had never heard her sing anything quite that way. The words grew louder with each line:

"And this be our motto: 'In God is our trust!'
And the star-spangled banner in triumph shall wave
O'er the land of the free..."

She paused for a moment after hitting the high note, as the "free" echoed throughout Wrigley Field.

Wow. If that doesn't send chills up everyone's spine, thought Austin, *then they aren't breathing.*

"…and the home of the brave!"

When Ashley finished, everybody still seemed to be soaking it in, as if they'd never heard anything like it. But then the ballplayers started to clap, and then the crowd, and they went on like that for a full minute, then two—a thunder of applause. Even the British sailors with Austin were clapping and cheering.

"Marvelous!" cried Leftenant Brumbley, slapping Austin on the back. "Your sister was smashing. Simply marvelous!"

Ashley had been marvelous, but no one in Normal would ever know how marvelous she could be unless Austin got her home—and soon. The clock was still ticking. The show over, the British sailors rose to their feet to load their cannons for yet another attack on Fort McHenry. After all, attacking Fort McHenry was their job.

"Do let me know if you hear of any openings elsewhere," a sailor said as he tugged at Austin's sleeve. "Any place off this ship. I'm even willing to be copied and pasted if that helps."

"Oh," Austin nodded. "Sure thing."

When he checked his watch, he nearly had a heart attack. Only five minutes left until Ashley was supposed to sing at the talent competition!

"I've got to get Ashley out of there now," he told himself. Only how?

Ashley was positive she hadn't stepped on any links, but all of a sudden she was acting like a puppet on a string.

"Hang on," she told Jessi. "I don't know what's going on, but—"

"But we're sure going to find out!"

Jessi flapped her arms as they tumbled out over the field. Not on, but *over*—and about twenty feet off the ground. The ballplayers waved as if they saw that kind of thing all the time. Fly balls maybe? Except fly balls don't disappear into the sky like they were doing.

They were foul by a mile.

"What if I'm afraid of heights?" asked Jessi.

Ashley could see the field below her feet growing smaller and smaller, like the view from a space-shuttle launch.

"Too late now!"

They would just have to hold on...but not for long. Because in less time than it would take to explain, the view started to change—from a ball field to a perky blue and yellow checkerboard. From outdoors to in. From a big Wrigley Field sign over center field to a flashing neon sign that said...

"Hey, Ashley, it's your name!"

Well, how about that! Ashley began to feel a soft floor beneath her feet as the new Web site came into focus. An info banner on the left had cute balloons to click on for more information. The balloons said stuff like:

Click Here for More on Chiddix Chargers Girls Gymnastics

Chargers Soccer. Yeah! Click for a Schedule

Ashley's Best Book Picks

Ashley's Fave Christian Music

My Family

Jessi began laughing as if she'd never stop.

"This is your Web site, Ash. Of all the places on the Internet, we're back on *your* site. Can you believe—"

"I know." Ashley only knew the parts Austin had shown her a couple of days ago when he'd still been working to finish the rest. "I just wonder who brought us here."

"Well, I don't know anything about that. But at least one thing's different here at *www-dot-AshleyWebster-dot-com*." Jessi crossed her arms.

"What's that?"

"Look down. You're not dressed up like somebody else in one of those wild costumes. You're not blind. You're not a rock star or Silas."

Jessi was right. Of all the Web sites they'd visited, this was the only one where Ashley could just be Ashley and no one else.

Cool.

But they still weren't home yet. For just a moment she remembered the keyboard she might never have.

And she sighed.

CHAPTER 19

Three-Minute Warning

⊕

Time on Austin's watch: 11:20.

Time left before Ashley was supposed to sing: Five minutes, tops.

"You're doing a fine job of helping your sister, Captain." Leftenant Brumbley patted Austin on the back. "Quite commendable. No need to look so glum."

The cannons kept spitting out horrible clouds of stink and cannonballs at Fort McHenry. Only now Austin didn't try to plug his nose or worry about the noise. He'd have to get used to it if he was going to be stuck on this Web site for the rest of his life.

"No, you don't understand," said Austin. "I *can't* do it."

"Can't do what?"

Ka-BOOOM!

"I thought I'd be able to follow her through the Web and find us a way back. But I can't even find my way out of this battle. I didn't know the control buttons to this site would be out of reach."

The leftenant squinted up at the sky. "Pity."

"I can't press Back, and I can't press Forward. I can't reach anything."

"Hmm." The leftenant appeared to study the Web-page controls Austin couldn't reach. They were probably about as high up as a third-story window. He looked at his cannon and rubbed his chin. "Perhaps a well-placed British cannonball might help, then?"

With only three minutes left, Austin sprinted down the nearly empty school hallway toward the auditorium. With his sister so far a no-show, they must have taken a short break before the big announcement, since everybody was heading back to their seats—everybody but a small group of girls standing by the double doors. One waved at the others to hurry back inside.

Naturally Tucker Campbell stood at the center of her fan club, her smile wide enough to cover for them all. And naturally the judges would be calling her name in just a few moments.

"Oh, Austin!" She noticed him. "There you are. No sign of Ashley, I assume?"

"Actually"—he huffed and puffed—"I found her."

He did his best not to smile at the cloud of panic that shadowed her face at his words.

"But she's still not here?" she asked, bringing back the smile.

Boy, she's practically a pro. "Not yet."

"Oh, good." She sighed, then caught herself. "I mean, that's too bad."

Austin didn't stop to explain anything. He checked to make sure the camera cable was connected to his laptop and the camera was fired up and ready to go. Then he handed a note to Jodie Hampton, one of Tucker's friends, and whispered in her ear, "Give this to my sister when you see her next, will you, please? It's important."

She couldn't know what he was talking about, but she nodded while her other two friends stood by as if they were waiting for the party to begin. Probably they thought it would pay to be close to Tucker, in line for the first hug when the winner was announced. Who knew? They might even get themselves into the newspaper photos.

Speaking of pictures, Austin was ready to take his.

"How about a quick shot for the Web site?" he asked, trying to look calm and cool.

Tucker flinched when Austin pulled out his camera, but she didn't move away quickly enough.

"Everybody say 'cheesecake.' "

Tucker couldn't help it. She'd been raised for this.

"Cheese—"

Flash!

He kind of wished Tucker had been standing there alone, so the other three girls wouldn't... Well, on second thought, maybe this had turned out perfectly. He stashed the camera in his backpack and watched the status bar at the bottom of his computer screen slowly turn red.

Two files, three, four. There. All downloaded. Now Austin just had to tie into the overhead projector in the auditorium— and quick. He pushed in through the double doors.

"Austin!" His parents caught sight of him from the middle of the crowd, but he couldn't stop now. He waved at them and hurried up the aisle to the front.

"Seeing as how our tenth finalist has not shown up for her mandatory performance"—Mr. Hayward stared as Austin came up the aisle, but he kept talking—"we have no choice but to award the top honors and the keyboard to—"

"Excuse me, sir." Austin really wished there was another way to do this than making a big scene. His sister was the actress, not him. Everyone turned to look at him, kind of like people would do if the pastor at a wedding said, "If anyone has cause that John and Susy should not be wed, let him speak now or forever hold his peace," and somebody actually spoke up.

"Austin Webster." Mr. Hayward narrowed his eyes at Austin, probably wishing he could make him disappear with a laser look.

But Austin couldn't be stopped.

Still holding his laptop, he climbed the steps to the stage and stepped right up to the microphones he'd wired for the singers. He winked at Drew back in the sound booth. All set.

"Ashley's on her way here," he announced. "Sort of."

"Sort of?" Mr. Hayward frowned and crossed his arms. "*Is* she on her way?"

Austin swallowed hard.

"It's kind of hard to explain, but if I can just show you on the big screen instead…"

Well, that created hubbub in the crowd. Mr. Hayward held up his hands for quiet as he turned to the judges sitting behind a table off to the side at stage right. Mayor Wurstheim leafed through a binder, stopped, and read a few pages. She shrugged her shoulders.

Austin wasted no time keying up the projector and the wireless connection. Surprise! There on the screen, bigger than life, was a sight no one else could have expected to see.

Tucker Campbell stood toe-to-toe next to his sister, live from *www.AshleyWebster.com*. And it didn't look as though they were having a friendly chat.

CHAPTER 20

CLueLess Judges

"Here they are." Austin smiled as he cranked up the volume so everyone in the audience could get an earful of Tucker Campbell's whining.

"I don't know what your sneaky brother is trying to prove," she shouted, only inches from Ashley's face, "but if he thinks he's going to keep me from winning *my* contest, he's *crazy!*"

The crowd murmured, probably trying to figure out where the girls were. Of course, Austin wasn't about to try to explain that one now. But he thought he saw Tucker's parents looking for the exit, probably hoping they could stop their daughter from saying whatever she might say next!

"And you know what else? You never had a chance, thanks to the way I handled your brother. And those clueless judges. Ha! They have no idea what happened to you, and isn't that a shame? We may both be here now—wherever here is—but *I* won the contest. And you'd better get used to it!"

Austin almost wished he hadn't done what he had. But who would believe he was to blame? Up on the big screen, Tucker's friends huddled in a corner almost out of view, looking totally confused. Who wouldn't be confused, their first time on the Internet?

Ashley stood there, letting Tucker make a total fool of herself. *Perfect.* Austin could tell she held his note in her hand. Jodie must have given it to her, the way Austin had asked.

Back in the auditorium, the judges were whispering to one another, taking out their clipboards, and erasing all kinds of things from their judging score sheets.

Way to go, Tucker, Austin thought.

But something wasn't quite right. Ashley had the note. She knew what to do. And she knew she couldn't be any later than she already was.

"Step on the e-mail link!" he whispered. His note told her which one. And if that didn't work, he had a Plan B. In any case, it was time for Ashley Webster to get back to Normal and step up to the microphone. It was time for his sister to win the prize. He'd been chasing her all over the Internet for this.

"Come on, Ashley!"

But Ashley still stood there; then she waved.

"I'm very sorry I can't make it today," she said loudly enough for everyone in the auditorium to hear. "But my brother says he's showing everything here to the audience at school. So I hope you can hear me. Hi, Mom and Dad! Don't worry about me."

That's it? Austin couldn't believe what he was hearing. No explanation? Just "I'm very sorry I can't make it"? Austin had no idea what had gotten into his sister.

Meanwhile, Tucker's mouth sagged open, and she brought her hands to her cheeks.

"You mean people can see us?" she squeaked.

Ashley nodded and waved again while Tucker looked as if she wanted to melt into the floor.

Austin knew the crowd had seen enough of the Tucker Campbell Show, and the judges were starting to get antsy. If Ashley couldn't come to the Greatest Young Vocalist Competition, then it was time for Plan B. He'd use the recording he'd made at the Chicago Cubs game, a sort of Ashley Webster music video. That would have to do.

So he piped Ashley's voice over the sound system. It rang out clear as a bell and stronger than he'd ever heard as she slowly sang the fourth stanza of the national anthem. A second later everyone could see her standing on the infield grass at Wrigley Field, singing her heart out.

You'd think that after hearing some of the best young singers in the state, people would have been used to great performances by now. But the words seemed to hit them just as they had hit the crowd at Wrigley Field. And pretty soon everybody in the auditorium was on their feet, hanging on every word. Never mind that Ashley wasn't actually there. Nobody seemed to care. Everyone loved her.

The hush at the end of her solo was followed by wild applause as soon as everyone had caught their breath. It got so noisy that Mayor Wurstheim had to hold up a hand to quiet people down. She held the rule book in her other hand.

"I can tell that you all enjoyed that song from Miss Webster."

Everyone started cheering all over again, and the mayor raised her hand once more.

"But…as chief judge of the Illinois Greatest Young Vocalist Competition, I regret to tell you that recorded or video entries are not acceptable. Finalists must compete in person."

After a few groans the auditorium went silent. Mayor Wurstheim went on to announce the winner. And it was no surprise who won the Yamaha Pro keyboard. The tall eighth grader from Peoria almost tripped on his way up the stage, but he was grinning so hard it didn't seem to bother him. By that time the audience had recovered enough to clap politely. Nobody had ever said he wasn't talented.

As for Tucker Campbell, she ended up taking third runner-up, which was basically fourth place. In all the excitement, Austin heard Mayor Wurstheim mumbling something to Mr. Hayward about "unsportsmanlike conduct." That and the crack about the clueless judges must have done it.

The mayor wasn't finished, though, and after whispering with all the judges, she returned to the microphone with a smile on her face. The clapping and whistling and cheering started all over again when she announced a special People's Choice award for…

Who else?

"Ashley Webster!"

Ashley's parents accepted the honor for her while everyone cheered. Mrs. Webster started crying, and Mr. Webster told everybody thanks and that he would be sure to pass along the award as soon as he found his daughter. Everyone thought that was a clever joke.

"I don't know how you made that recording, son"—Austin's dad pounded him on the back after they came down from the stage—"but that was something special."

"I know, Dad."

Then, as the photographers moved in to take pictures, his dad stopped, and a puzzled look came over his face.

"Come to think of it, are you sure that was Ashley's voice?"

"Are you kidding?" Austin slid through the crowd. "That was her all right."

He couldn't quite make the quick getaway he'd planned

though. His mom caught up to him just outside the back doors, out in the main hallway.

"Not so fast, Austin. You still need to explain a couple of things."

She was right. And he also had an e-mail to send to Ashley@AshleyWebster.com. With Ashley's help, he had a few more girls to rescue, which he could do now that (a) he knew exactly where they were, and (b) they could hit Reply to his e-mail. *No problem.*

"Well? I'm waiting," his mother said.

Austin looked up at her and started to tell her in three different ways. Finally he sighed.

"Okay, but you're never going to believe me."

The Hyperlinkz Guide to Safe Surfing

Austin T. Webster here, and at the end of this adventure, I'm going to do the educational thing all by myself, without any help from my sister.

Ashley: Even though you didn't actually visit a lot of the Web sites mentioned in *Web Jam*?

Austin: Where did you come from? I thought you were still hanging around *www.AshleyWebster.com* until we got everybody out.

Ashley: Two words, Austin: chat room. Don't you remember building one into my site? I'm chatting while I'm waiting.

Austin: Fine. But first of all let me explain to everybody that I really don't mind how much attention Ashley got in this adventure. After all, I'm a behind-the-scenes kind of guy. I can take it.

Ashley: Ah, he's noble.

Austin: Second of all, I should tell you there really is a Web site where you can find out almost anything about music. Actually, there's more than one. In fact, there's so much about music on the World Wide Web, well, you could spend years tracking it all down. Not that you'd want to. But if you ever have to write a school paper on classical music, for example, or Gregorian chant (an ancient kind of church music), you can type in the Web address *www.refdesk.com/music.html.* It's your open door to the world of music. Your portal. Your spring-board. Your jumping-off place. Your—

Ashley: I think they get the idea, Austin.

Austin: Hey, I'm just trying to explain, okay? Anyway, here's another cool site that's real, not made up just for this book: *www.nyise.org/fanny.* Don't try *www.FannyCrosbyHymns .com* because that was just the pretend Web address we used in the adventure.

Remember: *A lot of the Web sites we visit in our adventures are made up, so don't get upset if you can't find them!* But get this: Fanny Crosby was one of the most amazing Christian song-writers who ever lived. She lived from 1820 to 1915, and even though she was blind, she wrote the words to thousands of hymns. She lived to be fairly old and once said that if someone offered her sight, she wouldn't take it. "I might not have sung hymns to the praise of God," she said, "if I had been distracted by the beautiful and interesting things about me." Wow. Kind of reminds you of what Ashley learned in this story, doesn't it? Anyway, you can find out all about Fanny Crosby at the site I just told you about.

Oh, and remember how Fanny's friend stopped by her

house, in a hurry for her help with a song? It really happened that way, except, unlike Ashley, Fanny was able to come up with a great song for him in just a few minutes. That was just the way she was.

Ashley: Are you saying I'm no good at songwriting?

Austin: Not me! All I'm saying is that Fanny Crosby was awesome.

Ashley: And speaking of awesome, don't forget Paul.

Austin: Yeah, I'm just getting to him. One of the things you *won't* ever find on the Web is Paul's Greatest Hits. Remember Ashley's visit to the Macedonian prison where Paul and Silas were singing up a storm? Well, in our story it was Paul and Ashley. Point is, nobody knows exactly what their hymns sounded like, especially since Paul didn't exactly record any. We do know that psalms were popular song material though. Jewish people have always liked to put psalms to music. Besides that, Paul wrote about "psalms, hymns, and spiritual songs" in the book of Ephesians in the Bible. And Jesus probably sang a psalm at the Last Supper. That's why this adventure put the words of Psalm 56 in Paul's mouth—at least the Paul of the Web. Check out this psalm in your own Bible to see which verses he sang.

Ashley: How about a little more info on Francis Scott Key, the guy who wrote the national anthem?

Austin: Born 1779, died 1843. A lawyer and a poet, and active in his church. He even wrote a few hymns himself. He was also a very nice guy who went out of his way to help rescue Dr. William Beanes from the British during the invasion of 1814.

I would guess you don't know anybody who can recite the second, third, and fourth stanzas of our national anthem. Like, *"On the shore, dimly seen, through the mists of the deep, where the foe's haughty host, in dread silence reposes—"*

Ashley: Are you going to explain what a "haughty host" is? And what's the "reposes" stuff all about?

Austin: I was just getting started. You're going to have to look up those words in the dictionary. Because the next line goes—

Ashley: Stop already!

Austin: Okay, okay. Thanks to my sister I'm not going to write out all the words here, but I'll tell you what: It's your job to look up the second, third, and fourth stanzas of "The Star-Spangled Banner" at *www.bcpl.net/~etowner/anthem.html.* Keep a dictionary handy. There's some good info about Mr. Key at that site too. Like, did you know "The Star-Spangled Banner" borrowed an old English tune called "To Anacreon in Heaven" and just added Mr. Key's words? Also, "The Star-Spangled Banner" wasn't adopted by Congress as the American national anthem until 1931? And don't forget those lines in stanza four about praising and trusting God. The way I see it, a national anthem should reflect what a country stands for. Or should stand for.

Well, that should give you something to think about—or listen to. There's music all over the Internet. But a quick word of advice: You'll want to steer clear of a lot of music on the Internet. As in "no thanks." When you know where to look, there's plenty of good music to be found. A lot of it is just plain fun to listen to. Your folks might even have some good ideas about what you might want to listen to.

So where does that leave us? Singing, for sure. And the bigger job of explaining to our parents everything that's happened. Believe me, we're still working on that part of our adventure, but we'll let you know.

See ya,

Austin (and Ashley)

P.S. to parents: The Internet can be a lot of fun. But please make sure your child is surfing safely. That means being there for them. Know what they're accessing. And consider a good filtering service or software since it can help you sidestep some nasty surprises. We can't tell you to use one service over another, but you might start by checking out a great site called *www.filterreview.com*. It'll give you all the choices.

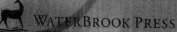

Please visit Robert Elmer's Web site at *www.RobertElmerBooks.com* to learn more about other books he's written or to schedule him to speak to your school or home-school group.